Signals

Seasons of Want and Plenty, Volume 2

Kris Farmen

Published by Blazo House, 2023.

This is a work of fiction. Similarities to real people, places, or events are entirely coincidental.

SIGNALS

First edition. April 4, 2023.

ISBN: 979-8215286371

Written by Kris Farmen.

For my girls, Jaclyn and Naia.

1

REUNION — A NEW ASSIGNMENT — COLONIAL HISTORY — ICE SKATING PARTY — HOT PURSUIT— LIFE LESSONS — HITTING BOTTOM — LACK OF COMMUNICATION — MARVELOUS MODERN TECHNOLOGY — THE COMPANY WILL TAKE EVERYTHING FROM YOU — A SMART LITTLE CREOLE — HOW DO YOU SAY THIS IN RUSSIAN — THUMBS-UP — ADAMS EXAMINES THE KALE

There are few things in life more awful than the sight of a child-sized grave. Ivan Lukin's daughter Anastasia from his first marriage—his only surviving child—stood next to him in the graveyard of Fort St. Michael overlooking the Bering Sea coast. The tundra wind whipped her hair out from beneath the shawl over her head and flapped the hem of her skirts around her calves. She was sixteen years old and just two days before had been delivered back to him from the colony's parochial school in the capital of New Archangel. It was the same institution Lukin himself had attended in his formative years. He had not seen her since she was eleven.

They had been standing there for some time, watching the Russian America Company's supply ship pull away, bound across the ocean on the second half of its annual voyage around the globe, back to St. Petersburg. The August sky had been overcast for days but the clouds were breaking up and beams of sunlight shot down from the heavens to cast blotches of shadow and light across the water as the tall ship cut its wake through the waves. Anything to keep from looking at little Ilya's grave and the three-barred Orthodox cross that marked it.

"I gave the cross a new coat of paint back in May," Lukin said after a while. "I do it every year."

Anastasia didn't move her eyes from the ship. Ilya had been her half brother, born to Lukin by his current wife Iriana, and Lukin could only guess at what scant memories she had of him. He himself had been fourteen when he was returned to his parents at Fort Kolmakov on the Kuskokwim River. After the hugs and tears of the initial reunion the experience of being shoved back into his previous life had been both bewildering and alienating by turns.

"He was only two when I left," Anastasia said.

"He was, yes."

Her mouth turned into the faintest of smiles. "I remember you two used to hide under a blanket and whisper and giggle. You always called it the blanket house."

Lukin had been holding himself together but suddenly felt tears pooling in his eyelids. He laughed quietly at the memory but couldn't speak.

"How did God take him?" she asked. Her voice was distant, as if spoken to the ship moving across the sea, or perhaps to the wind itself.

He cleared his throat, blinking away the water. "He took ill with fever at Nulato right after I got back from the trip to Fort Youcon. He managed to fight it off, but then when we returned here after the start of winter the fever came back."

"Just like Dmitri." Her older brother had also died of an unknown illness at the age of four, many years ago when they still lived at Fort Kolmakov on the Kuskokwim River. Back before everything started falling apart. It felt like another world entirely.

"Yes," Lukin whispered. "Just like Dmitri."

"And Iriana no longer lives with you?"

"She keeps some things at the house." Every now and then she would show up at the door, usually drunk, and attempt to spend the night. Usually it only took a few minutes before she started lecturing Lukin on everything he'd done wrong in his life. The rest of the time she spent in the arms of Mikhail Stepanov, the current St. Michael fort manager. In the colonial Russian his title was Bidarshik, and the title seemed to be the primary thing she was interested in.

"My dear, could you look at me?"

Anastasia obliged.

"I know from firsthand experience how hard it is to be home from school. You've been gone so many years and you've changed so much, and the people back home just seem like the same old folks."

She lifted her eyebrows a little in agreement.

"I was there myself once," Lukin said. "And we both need to be patient with one another."

She nodded, then turned back to Ilya's grave and made the sign of the cross. While away at school she had taken to wearing long, delicate gloves that she sewed herself to hide the puckered pink scars of the burns she'd received the day her mother died. She put them on when she first got out of bed, and she didn't take them off until she blew out the last candle at night. Lukin pursed his lips, then bowed his head and joined her in silent prayer.

When they turned to leave, Yosif Denisov stood at the fence gate waiting for them. "Stepanov sent me to find you."

"What for?" Lukin asked as he held the gate open for his daughter to exit.

"He has an assignment for you."

"An assignment."

"For all of us, really." Denisov was the second in command at Fort Nulato, deep in the colony's interior along the River Kwifpak. He and Lukin had known each other since they were children, and in fact had almost died together.

* * *

There was an old story in Russian America that when the Czar sent his Imperial Navy to remove the colony's first governor Aleksandr Baranov for his abuse of the Native people, the new governor—a naval officer, family man, and avid ice skater—noticed immediately that the children in the wake of the tyranny his predecessor had inflicted had no toys or other means to amuse themselves. Determined to remedy this, he took his sword to the blacksmith and had him cut it up and turn it into the first pair of ice skates in the capital, which he gave to a young girl of mixed Russian and Aleut parentage. From then on, every child who entered the school at New Archangel was given a pair of ice skates at the governor's expense. They were crude by the measure of the outside world, just basic steel blades riveted to wooden lasts that you strapped onto your shoes with buckles. But they worked and they were the only skates most of the kids knew.

Just inside the edge of the dank evergreen rainforest behind the capital were a series of lakes, and on cold blue-sky winter days when everything froze hard there was a standing ice-skating party among the children after school. Young Lukin and Denisov stepped lively along the boardwalk with their skates hung over their shoulders. Down the main street of the town, past the Company offices and warehouses, the officers' club and the bakery, all built of logs and painted yellow with red trim. The spaces between were filled with stumps, random wood chips, and mud frozen hard like concrete. Piles of cordwood stood in every available space.

Down at the waterfront a sloop had been careened on the kelp-strewn gravel and a work gang was scraping down her hull. The men had a fire going and had to keep dousing the boat with warmed seawater to keep the barnacles from freezing to the planking. The smoke and the cloud of their collective breath turned amber in the winter sunlight and you could hear the scraping and the lewd talk carried on the chilly air.

The scent of the cold sea came in with every breath. Sava Golinov, a friend of theirs, was already out ahead of them and he looked back with a wave as he disappeared into the edge of the woods. A trio of young Kolosh women, let inside the town's palisade for the day, approached them on the boardwalk. These were the Aboriginal inhabitants of the rain-soaked islands. The girls' fathers and uncles had fought Baranov and his men to a draw thirty years before with guns and axes bought from the British and they made only the scantest of eye contact with Lukin and Denisov. They were barefoot on the cold planks and naked save for the cedar-bark skirts they wore under the Hudson Bay blankets they'd wrapped around their shoulders. On their heads were the standard Chinese-looking hats woven from spruce roots. They moved into single file and Lukin fell in behind Denisov so they could pass by. All wore carved wooden disks pushed into wide slits cut in their lower lips; the weight of the wood pulled their lips down to display their teeth, and the whole arrangement jiggled as they walked. Even after two years in the capital, young Lukin found it hard not to stare at this. Among other things, there was the eternal question of how they ate soup with such ornamentation.

Denisov turned and pinched his own lower lip out, wobbling it to and fro while crossing his eyes.

"Making sport of your own people?" Lukin said. Denisov's father and mother were both of mixed Kolosh and Russian parentage who'd relocated to Fort St. George on the Gulf of Kenay.

"They're Sitka Kolosh," Denisov said. "My mother's people are Yakutat Kolosh. I'll make fun of Sitka people all I want."

The network of boardwalks ended once you were outside the stockade. New Archangel was ringed by an immense stump field and the cavernous cedar-plank houses of the local Kolosh occupied one end of this clearing down near the beach. Hundreds of dugout canoes were turned over on the dead grass just above the sand. Here and there stood the dovetailed log houses of mixed Russian and Kolosh families, a mix known as Creole in the colony. Two-thirds of the people resident in New Archangel were Creoles of some sort, including Lukin who was half Dinneh from the Interior, a quarter Koniag from Kodiak Island, and a quarter Russian.

Inside the dark world of the spruce and hemlock trees, the path to the skating pond wound between mossy stumps and rootwads thrown up when their trunks had been toppled by winter storms. Dormant stalks of devil's club curled up from the forest floor like giant gnarled fingers covered in quarter-inch spines.

The lake appeared as a lightening of the air in the forest ahead, then as they approached it widened into shape as a broad expanse of ice that caught the blue color of the sky like a mirror and reflected the shape of the mountains beyond. There were already a dozen kids on the ice, with more at the shore, Sava included, buckling on their skates. They kept a supply of firewood at the lake covered over with a tarp, and someone had gotten a fire going for warming up. Further out on the lake, toward the middle, an ice-cutting crew was at work. A Russian teamster piloted a pair of draft horses, dragging a cutting rig on runners with a saw blade that bit into the ice as they walked back and forth in a chessboard pattern. Two Kolosh workers moved after him, breaking out each two-foot cube with axes and prybars and lifting them onto straw they'd scattered to keep them from refreezing to the surface. Lukin had heard that ice was becoming one of the Company's main exports; they shipped it all over the Pacific coast and even to Hawaii and Australia.

Lukin and Denisov sat down on a log to get their skates on just as Sava stood up. "Lubina and Tatyana are here," he said, lifting his eyebrows. They were the twin daughters of the Company's chief in-country accountant, a man from Irkutsk named Tardikov. They were the only white girls close to their age in town, and the object of every boy's unspoken desire.

They followed Sava onto the ice and glided out to where the skating party was playing Boaire. The version played in the colony had the children divided into two lines, boys versus girls, with each team linked hand-in-hand. "Send us a groom to take up our broom!" the girls called over. One of the boys skated out hard, trying to smash through the girls' line. Both sides whooped and shouted as the phalanx bent with his impact. The girls struggled to stay upright, but the line held. This meant the unsuccessful lad had to join their team as a groom. Then it was the boys' turn to call for a bride. The Tardikova girls were always the first to be called over, having blonde hair and womanly figures.

Denisov moved out to join the boys' side just as Tatyana pushed off with her face clamped down in concentration. She got her shoulder down and rammed into the joint between two of the smaller boys' hands, a strategic decision on her part, Lukin supposed. For his part, he preferred to skate alone.

He was fond of skating fast, often doing circuits of the lake while the others stayed within sight of the fire. Tatyana made it through the line, which meant she got to pick her groom and drag him over to join the girls. Naturally the biggest strongest boys were desired. As they shouted back and forth over her choice Lukin dug his skates deep into the wind-burnished ice and took off, building speed with each kick. Over the course of many sessions he'd worked it out that when going around the contours of the shore he could lean into his turns and swing his outside arm like a pendulum to gather extra speed. The spruce growing right down to the bank peeled away as he rounded the first bend, a visual effect he enjoyed immensely.

Lukin hurled himself in and around the bends to the far end of the lake. Behind him the shouting faded away until there was only the cut of his blades and the sound of his breath. But when he glanced over his shoulder he was startled to see Tatyana coming after him, followed by her sister and a pack of girls, with Sava and Denisov racing to overtake them. Evidently she had her sights set on Lukin as a groom. He may not have been playing, but if you were on the ice you were fair game.

He pushed harder with each stroke of the skates, moving so fast he could feel the wind lift his hair from his coat collar. Tatyana and another girl cut him off and tried to clothesline him onto the ice but Lukin hunkered down just enough to duck under their linked arms and shot right between them. Lubina Tardikova tried to grab his coat but Sava slid between them, grinning like some dopey knight errant as he pushed her off balance.

Lukin worked his skates to build his speed back up. Another glance behind him showed the girls still coming, all laughing and shouting except Tatyana, who, more so than the others, looked like she meant business. He knew he could hold the curves better than anyone there, so he bent his path around a long, forested peninsula, swinging his outside arm and dropping his inside fingertips to the glossy ice as he'd seen older skaters do.

Two of his pursuers lost their grip and fell with muffled thumps. Three more girls were still upright but had to swing their turn too wide and ended up way off course. When he dared look over there was Denisov at his side with enough presence of mind to drop him a sly wink. The shouting behind them rose to a crescendo, but it was only when they moved their eyes forward again that they saw the ice cutter and the horses, right there in front of them. Lukin screamed as the team reared back in their traces, then both he and Denisov toppled sideways, sliding bodily over the ice directly under the animals' feet. All they could do was wrap their arms around their heads pray they didn't get stomped on. One hoof shod in iron spikes for grip on the ice came down right in front of Lukin's nose. That hoof had a split that had been closed up with brass staples, a detail he recalled for a long time afterward.

The teamster swore as the horses jumped again and threw their heads. Lukin had lost track of where Denisov was. When his momentum finally gave out he rose to his knees, trembling and looking for his friend. The teamster, still swearing, set the ice brake and got down to calm the animals. Neither Denisov nor the two workmen were anywhere to be seen but then a hand gripped his collar and yanked him to his feet. Kolosh curses blasted into his ear and he twisted around to gain a fearful sight of one of the workers, a man in a Hudson Bay blanket and a spruce-root hat. Half his face was covered with intricate tattoos that stopped in a vertical line down the bridge of his nose and halfway across his mouth. A heavy copper ring with small bangles hung from his septum. His partner wore the standard spruce-root hat and an old blue tailcoat with a necklace of Chinese coins over his chest. They smelled of fish, woodsmoke, and grease. Both wore slippers made of old blankets for traction on the ice.

"Watch where you're going, kid!" the one in the tailcoat said in Russian. The driver stood in front of the horses, stroking their noses and speaking softly to them.

The man with the tattooed face pulled Lukin up so his ear was almost at his lips, then hissed something directly into his skull.

"He says his favorite thing to eat is soup made of boiled Creole kids. With a spoonful of seal oil in the bowl." He favored Lukin with an unfriendly smile as he translated. Young Lukin was so terrified he nearly peed his trousers.

"Let him go," said the teamster. "He's learned his lesson." Finally Lukin caught sight of Denisov standing nearby as the tattooed man lowered him back to the ice. Everyone else had assembled in a crowd a few rods distant, watching. It was not the best of days.

* * *

The American ship banged her keel against the shallow bottom of the Bering Sea every time a wave bore her down. Lukin stood at the open bidara's tiller, watching with the oarsmen as the cold rain lashed their faces and dripped from their seal-gut raincoats.

The ship rose, then crested, then slammed down again. Lukin winced.

"Jesus, that looks painful," said Hakrin, a Finlander. He was a new company recruit, assigned to Lukin's crew after one of his oarsmen died of a tooth abscess. All the sailors on the ship's deck staggered about, holding on to whatever they could find and trying to keep their feet.

Lukin and his crew had been ordered out from Fort St. Michael when the sail was sighted to guide the vessel into the harbor. It was a notoriously shallow place for ships, and rough weather like this made it nearly impossible to bring them in.

"Only a fool would try to pilot a ship into St. Michael in September," Hakrin said. He sat only three feet away from Lukin but had to shout over the wind. He fidgeted with the rawhide lacings that held the boat's walrus skin shell taut over the wooden frame. This bothered Lukin in the extreme, but as a boat captain he knew it was best to pick your battles.

"Maybe so," he replied, looking up at the cloudy sky, "but they came all the way from San Francisco. They would have had to set out in April."

"You said they're here to string a telegraph wire?"

"That's what the bidarshik told me." No-one riding in the boat knew anyone who had ever received a telegram, and Lukin had only the most rudimentary understanding of what it was.

"There's talk that they are spies from the United States Army."

"You shouldn't believe everything you hear, Hakrin. Rumors fly like bats at dusk here in Russian America."

"If they hit any rocks on the bottom they'll start breaking up," said a half-Malimiut Creole named Pamilan.

Lukin watched as the ship wallowed forward on shortened sails. He'd put out from shore on a beam reach but there was no way to close the final distance by sail without risking a nasty collision. "Let's furl the canvas, boys," he ordered. "And put out your oars."

Hakrin and Pamilan got the sail tucked in and made fast, then lifted the mast out of its collar, no mean feat in the wind and pitching sea. They lashed it down and returned to their seats. That done, all six crewmen stood against their oars as they dipped down into a trough, then came up the other side. Salt spray whipped against them. One of the forward rowers, a Koryak tribesman from Kamchatka, suddenly twisted over the rail and vomited his breakfast into the sea. Lukin had to lean hard on the tiller to compensate for the lack of thrust on that side of the boat while he retched and gagged.

"Back at your oar, Yuri!" he shouted as the Koryak slumped back in his seat. "Dig hard, damn you!" The wind stole the bite of his words from his mouth, making them barely audible. Yuri dragged a sleeve across his mouth and wrapped his fingers back around his oar. Lukin squinted against the wind and rain, feeling more than a little queasy himself.

Over on the ship, sailors were climbing into the rigging. They worked their way along the spars, pulling in more canvas. Lukin hoped they could keep out enough sheeting to maintain steerage. The last thing he wanted was to bring out more boats and try to tow them through this weather.

It took the boat a long twenty minutes to come up alongside the Yankee bark. An officer came to the rail and leaned over with a megaphone. Lukin cupped his hands around his lips, yelling, "Do you speak any Russian?"

The officer looked shoreward at the distant fort, then held up an index finger before hurrying away. He returned a moment later with a sailor in heavy oilskins.

"You speak any Russian?" Lukin called again.

"Yes," the sailor shouted down.

"We're here to guide you into the harbor. How much water does your vessel draw?"

The ship's bow went down and banged into the seabed yet again with a WHUMP you could hear over the wind. The officer and sailor were thrown to the deck. Shouts and English curses sounded from all quarters. Pamilan pointed aloft and Lukin gasped when he saw a man dangling from the clewline along one of the high spars. All eyes watched as he started moving hand over hand toward the mast where one of his mates helped him onto the relative safety of the ratlines.

The Russian-speaking sailor was back at the rail. "Three English fathoms," he called through the megaphone. His thick accent made the words difficult to parse. But three fathoms was too much to make it into the south end of the canal in such heavy seas. They would have to ride at anchor, assuming they could find somewhere where they weren't dragging their keel.

"Follow us around to the north," Lukin shouted, curving his hand around in an arc to indicate the bend of the coastline. "You won't make it into the harbor in this weather. We'll take you to the lee of the island where it's a little deeper and you can drop anchor until the weather backs down."

The ship's side heaved down toward the boat's gunwale. Shouting and cursing, Pamilan and the men on the port side yanked their oars from the locks and set them against the planking to push back their own boat before it got clipped and rolled them all into the ugly gray sea.

Between the Yankee sailor's poor Russian and the roar of the wind Lukin had to repeat his instructions three times before he was understood. The sailor translated for the officer, who in turn shouted a question as the skin boat bobbed up next to them on the following crest, so high relative to the ship that Lukin could have reached out and shaken his hand.

"Is there deeper place?" the sailor asked through the megaphone as they were carried down again. "Place where we no hit bottom?"

"Yes. We have a good spot. When you've made anchor, we'll have to load the men and supplies into our boat and lighter them to shore. Do you understand?"

"Yes. We follow and unload into small boat."

"Alright then." Lukin waved at the officer to follow. He heard orders being called on the deck, then the shrill report of the bosun's whistle. Lukin's crew dipped their oars and pulled away. Slowly, they moved around to the lee side of the island where the waves laid down and the whitecaps subsided just enough that it didn't feel like they were courting death. First Lukin noticed that the land didn't disappear every time their bow dipped down, then it became calm enough that he could stand at the tiller instead of crouching against the thwart. It was still choppy, but manageable.

He triangulated their position offshore by the only landmarks available on the flat, treeless coast—a very low rise to the southeast and the flagpole of the fort to the southwest. He had to squint through the weather to see them both.

"Hold up," he ordered the crew.

They needed no encouragement to stop rowing. Behind them, the American ship lumbered on, pitching against the bottom every few waves until she entered the line of the smoother water. The men aloft let out more canvas to catch the reduced wind, but at least she was off the bottom. Still, her keel likely had only two or three feet of clearance.

The ship cruised past them, maybe fifty yards out. Yuri was slouched over his oar, staring vacantly at the floorboards. The ashy green pallor of his face indicated someone who was having serious second thoughts about his chosen career.

The mate returned to the rail with the sailor. Lukin again cupped his hands to his mouth. "Drop your anchor anywhere out here!"

He watched the ship as more men were sent aloft to help pull in the last of the sheets. An extra sea anchor was tossed over the stern to slow them further, and there came the rattling of a heavy anchor chain. Six cormorants streaked past, flying low over the sea with the hard tailwind. Between the boat and the shore a raft of puffins floated with the utmost tranquility in the rolling waves. It was just another day for them.

Yuri's eyes met Lukin's for just a moment. Lukin moved forward and hunkered down next to him. "How are you holding up?"

The Koryak didn't answer.

"You'll feel better when you push through the nausea." Lukin reached under his raincoat—a kamleik, as it was called—and withdrew a flask of rum from the inside pocket of his jacket. He unscrewed the cap and offered it. Yuri shook his head.

"Probably a wise choice." Lukin handed the flask to Hakrin. "For strength and courage, lads. We have a lot of weight to land today."

Hakrin lifted the flask. "Strength and courage, Captain." He lifted the flask to his lips and took a healthy pop. Behind them, the ship's anchor plunged into the sea. Hakrin passed the flask and the rum made the rounds and when it came back Lukin saluted his boatmen and took his drink. Behind them, a voice was hailing in English.

When they came alongside again a rope ladder was rolled over the side. The sailor who spoke bad Russian came down first, followed by a man in a blue wool uniform trimmed in gold braid.

"What is your name?" Lukin asked the sailor.

"Hollister," he said. He indicated the small, spare-looking man just reaching the end of the ladder and trying without much success to time his dismount into the rolling boat. "This is Major Kennicott. He is boss."

The English names sounded thick and foreign when Lukin tried to wrap his tongue around them. The *h* sound didn't exist in Russian, and the sailor's name came out sounding something more like *Kowlitser*.

Kennicott finally made it down into the boat but had to plant a hand on a boatman's shoulder to steady himself. He shook Lukin's hand with a torrent of English. Up on the deck of the ship there were a dozen men waiting their turn to come down. Lukin noted that it would take two trips to get them all, and probably two more for their supplies. Maybe three or four.

"He asks if you are boss at fort," Hollister said. He was apparently not acquainted with the term bidarshik and must have learned his Russian on the other side of the Empire.

"Mikhail Stepanov is the bidarshik," Lukin replied.

Hollister looked confused.

"Bidarshik," Lukin repeated. "The boss."

"Ah. You take Yankees to Stepanov?"

"Yes." Another man came down the rope ladder, with another waiting to go. Each had his personal duffel slung over his shoulder. These were dropped into the boat before they stepped off. All of them wore blue wool uniforms that looked to Lukin's eye like military issue, notwithstanding Stepanov's assertion to Lukin that the expedition was privately funded and not a military venture.

There were no seats for them so they sat cross-legged on the floorboards and you could see from the way they hunched into themselves that the cold fall wind was cutting right through their clothes. They huddled together, looking down at their boots and blowing into their cupped hands while gawking at the skin boat, the crew, and the distant stripe of land as Hakrin and Pamilan set the mast in place, hoisted the canvas, and they drove for the northern mouth of the canal.

* * *

Anastasia had just finished digging out the last of the potatoes from their garden when Lukin came walking up the path from the fort to take his lunch. She piled them into her apron and carried them over to the wooden barrel that would be stored in the cellar and carefully dumped them onto the rest of the harvest. He came up to the driftwood fence and stood with his hands resting on the railing. The salad greens were done for the year save for a few resolute kale stems that continued to push out new growth in the waning sun. She still had to pull the carrots, kohlrabi, and turnips. The cabbages had been cut the previous week right when the first frosts came.

"Hello, Papa," she said, dusting off her gloved hands. Out here in the garden she wore a more plain set of gloves stitched from leather, but like all the others they extended up her arms most of the way to her elbows.

"Hello, Ermine."

She planted her hands on her hips with the thumbs pointing forward and Lukin couldn't help but think she was going to be on the make for a husband before long. The prevailing wisdom was that when girls returned from school it was time to marry them off, but Lukin couldn't quite bring himself to part from his only surviving child.

"Did you see Iriana anywhere down there?" she asked.

She'd never known Iriana as a stepmother beyond the couple years before she'd left for school, and had never really thought of her as such, so far as Lukin could tell. But his wife's departure for the bed of the new St. Michael bidarshik Stepanov was an endless font of gossip. Anastasia had more or less stepped right into that when she got off the boat. It certainly shifted the limits of Lukin's perspective to see how difficult things must have been for his own parents when he'd finally been shipped back to Fort Kolmakov.

The days were growing short and he disliked Fort St. Michael and its flat treeless tundra and shitty weather as much as ever. There didn't seem to be any end to things beyond death.

"I saw her tossing some dishwater out their door," Lukin said. "She didn't look my way."

Anastasia closed the garden gate behind her. He had a forlorn hope that she might hook her arm through his like a dutiful daughter and pat his hand and tell him everything would be all right, but instead she just flattened her lips and started for the house. "I've been warming the leftover fish pie from last night," she called over her shoulder.

Lukin looked back out at the water where you could just see the ship riding in the bay. The Yankees down at the beach were working to get their tents up while others appeared to be cooking lunch. The grassy flat above the beach was piled high with crates and boxes, and he'd been told this was only a fraction of what needed to be brought in from the ship. A chilly gust of wind whipped crossways across the tundra. It carried the scent of snow.

Inside, Anastasia drew off her work gloves and donned a pair made from fine fawnskin. She opened the pitchka door and pulled out the steaming pie, then filled a kettle and stuffed kindling into the coals to make a fast boil. Lukin was glad to be out of the wind and smiled at her as she set one of their porcelain cups down in front of him as the water began to hiss.

"How is it going with the unloading?" she asked, moving the pie away from the pitchka to cool off.

"It's crazy. The Yankees only have one man who can speak Russian, and not very well at that."

"Wouldn't they want to bring a few men who can speak Russian?"

"You would think so, but sadly."

"Stepanov has you serving as their guide," Anastasia said. "But how are you to do that if you cannot communicate with them?" She seemed slightly incredulous at the stupidity of it, and Lukin couldn't really blame her.

"We shall see. I speak five languages but none of them is English."

She sliced the leftover pie into two pieces and slid them onto plates painted with Chinese patterns in blue. He'd ordered them from the Company and paid with some of the gold he'd been awarded for spying on the British at Fort Youcon. He'd hoped they might soften Iriana's heart a little but now they just seemed irredeemably fancy. He regretted spending the money, but his daughter seemed enchanted by them.

"And you're taking them to Nulato?" She set one of the plates down in front of him with a fork and dippered him some water from a barrel into a tin cup.

"Nulato and all over creation, it sounds like. This Western Union Company—" the English words hung in the air like a foreign smell, "—is stringing the telegraph cable all the way across Siberia, then under the Bering Sea and up the Kwifpak. They plan to run it into Rupert's Land and then down to San Francisco."

She sat down across the table from him. "I wouldn't think they'd have you guiding them to San Francisco."

Lukin actually laughed a little. "No, Ermine, I wouldn't think so either. But they need someone who knows his way around the Kwifpak."

The kettle started to whistle. Anastasia rose and poured the hot water into the cups of zavarka. "Sounds to me like maybe the Company wants you to keep an eye on them. I've heard they're here as spies."

"Yes, I've heard that rumor as well. But what on earth would the United States want to spy on here?" He blew on a forkful of pie to cool it down. "Their government in Washington just spent four years dealing with that rebellion over the Negro slaves, and I should think they would have better things to do than spy on us." He drank the water from his tin cup in a single draught then traded it for the finer cup of tea. "In any event, the Company has directed Stepanov and all the other bidarshiks to give the Yankees any assistance possible with their expedition."

They began eating in silence, then Anastasia said, "I met some Yankees in Sitka. They're very loud."

Lukin had noticed since her return that his daughter had the habit of calling the capital Sitka instead of New Archangel, and he wasn't sure what to make of that. Sitka in his mind was the Kolosh name of the hill on which the governor's mansion stood, the spot where Baranov had made his stand against their assault back in 1805. not the town itself.

"Sailors, you mean?" he said around another mouthful of pie. Merchant ships from the United States regularly called at the capital, especially since Mexico had ceded California. In fact, more and more Yankee-made items had been finding their way into Russian America. The Company could buy its merchandise much more cheaply from them now that they were firmly established on the Pacific coast. The iron skillet that Anastasia had used to bake the pie in came from the United States and was marked with indecipherable Latin letters. The flour for the crust had been sourced in Oregon.

"Yes," Anastasia said. "One of the captains gave me and Gavrila some saltwater taffy." Gavrila was a girlfriend of hers from school; judging from the frequency with which she mentioned her it was plain that Anastasia missed her terribly.

"Saltwater taffy?" More exotic words.

"It's a kind of candy. It's soft and chewy like spruce gum, but sweet. And it melts in your mouth."

Not for the first time Lukin was struck by how worldly and erudite his baby girl had become. A certain pride collected in his breast, manifested as, *That's my daughter.*

"What, Papa?"

"Nothing, Ermine."

"Do you think they can do it?"

"Do what?"

"String the telegraph wire all that way."

He shrugged. "I guess we'll find out. But it sounds like a fool's errand to me."

"There's a telegraph line across the United States," Anastasia said. "And they've been trying to lay an undersea cable under the Atlantic Ocean between Europe and the Americas. They keep messing it up, though, so I bet they're trying the long way round the globe to see if they can make that work." She stirred a little sugar into her tea and took a long drink.

Stepanov had explained this to Lukin already, but it was impressive to hear it from Anastasia. "How'd you get so smart?"

She held a palm out and shrugged, a gesture he recognized as coming directly from him. It was something he'd picked up from his own father. "Just talking to the Yankee sailors."

Lukin frowned and leaned over the table another inch. "Just how much time did you spend around these sailors?"

"Papa, relax. They're just fun to talk to. The United States is an interesting country."

"So I'm told."

"But think about what this telegraph line will mean when they finally finish it. Being able to send a message around the world at the touch of a finger. And if the line comes through St. Michael, we'll be right next to it. You could get your assignments directly from the Company offices in an instant, instead of having to wait for a ship to deliver them around the world once a year. Would that not be wonderful?"

"Mmm." *Wonderful* was not the word Lukin would have used to describe such a circumstance. He chewed and swallowed another bite of the pie.

Anastasia waggled her fork between her thumb and forefinger. "Do you still think there's any chance the Company will set you up at Nuklukayet as a bidarshik?"

He looked up at her. The Company had been dangling this choice assignment in front of his face for several years now. Nuklukayet—a nearly impossible name for outsiders to pronounce—was a summer meeting place for all the Dinneh tribes of the colony's vast Interior. It was Russian soil, but the British Hudson Bay Company had been buying furs there illegally for nearly ten years. Their home base of Fort Youcon was also built illegally, which was why the colony's previous governor had sent Lukin up there to gather intelligence.

"I would expect," said Anastasia, "that if there's a telegraph line going up that way the Company will need to have a presence there. And the British will have to be pushed back over the 141st meridian."

Lukin sighed and pushed his empty plate away with lifted eyebrows. "Who knows?"

* * *

Mikhail Stepanov stood by the pile of American freight on the beach with Major Kennicott when Lukin trudged back from the house to reunite with his crew. The two bosses appeared to be examining the large wooden spools of wire they had landed on their final trip before lunch. The wind had fallen away to a light breeze, but the sea was still gray and rough and you could hear a knee-high surf breaking on the gravel shore outside the canal entrance.

Stepanov was a tall lanky man who had formerly been an army officer. When he came closer Lukin saw Iriana standing at his other side, handing around pastries from a plate to the Americans. Stepanov plucked the last one and Iriana pointedly didn't look at Lukin as she moved away. Stepanov's eyes shifted to watch her leave, then he broke his pastry in two and handed one half to Lukin.

"No, thank you," he said to his boss. The Company, it seemed, would take everything from you, even your wife.

Stepanov shrugged and bit into the half he'd offered. Hollister came around one of the stacks of crates. Kennicott asked him something which he translated to Stepanov as, "He asks how much longer getting gear."

The bidarshik looked over at Lukin.

"How much more cargo do they have?" Lukin asked. The hard part was forcing himself to give a shit.

Hollister's response didn't make any sense until he repeated it. "Twenty thousand funts."

"That's a lot of weight to move," Lukin said to Stepanov.

"It is."

"And we have only the one boat we can use?"

Stepanov pointed up the beach to where two of the Americans looked to be hard at work assembling some sort of ultra-modern craft. "The Yankees have brought a steam launch. Once they get it put together they can do the lightering."

"How soon do you foresee that happening?"

"Their engineer says he will have it together by midafternoon."

Pamilan and Hakrin and the others had untied the shorelines and were holding the boat's bow, ready to go. Their breath steamed in the chilly air while they waited. Down here at the beach the ship in the bay was hidden from view. Seagulls started their afternoon chorus, standing in a flock in the gathering light.

"Why not just wait, then?"

One side of Stepanov's mouth turned up ever so slightly. "Let us just say I will believe it when I see it. But until then I want you to keep bringing their things to shore. The sea ice will come any day now and their ship must return to San Francisco with all possible speed."

For maybe the thousandth time, Lukin wanted to smack Stepanov across the face, but this seemed unwise. Perhaps he should have challenged the man to a duel—it was, after all, his right as Iriana's husband—but what purpose would such a thing serve? It wasn't as if he and Iriana could actually be happy together. So instead he just said, "Very good, sir." He turned to Hollister. "You're with me."

"No," said Stepanov. "I need this man here on shore."

"Then how am I to communicate with the Yankee ship?"

"You're a smart little Creole. I'm sure you will figure something out."

Kennicott caught Stepanov's attention and spoke at length, pointing at the spools of wire and the crates, then out in the direction of the ship. He was clearly agitated.

Hollister translated. "He says things here you bring in morning are not things they need now. He wants you bring—" his voice trailed off. He cursed once in English, then mumbled something to himself. It took a great deal of effort for Lukin to not roll his eyes, a feat he could only accomplish by staring dully at their nearly worthless translator, whose limited services he was apparently not going to enjoy during the coming afternoon.

Fucking Stepanov, he thought. When the Bidarshik got drunk he loved to rail against the favored position Creoles held in the colony. He'd made no secret of his resentment that, unlike ethnic Russians, they paid no taxes to the Czar. It was a point of contention shared by many of the white workmen. And like many of his Russian workers, he openly hated the fact that not a few of these mongrels—as he made a point of calling them when in his cups—were placed by the Company in positions of authority over white men.

Lukin never did learn what it was Kennicott wanted them to bring. He'd finally just said fuck it and walked away with Hollister still fumbling around for the words. He and his crew were just getting ready to launch when a young-looking kid in one of the blue uniforms trotted up.

"What do you want?" he asked the kid.

The youth reached between Hakrin and Yuri and tapped the bow of the boat. "How do you say this in Russian?"

"Say what in Russian?" Lukin snapped.

"How do you say this in Russian?"

Lukin spread out his palms in exasperated incomprehension. The kid said something in English and made to climb aboard. He moved his hands to encompass the entire boat. "How do you say this in Russian?"

This time Lukin did roll his eyes. His lunch had him feeling sleepy and wishing for a nap, followed by maybe a leisurely afternoon of wingshooting ptarmigan and picking cranberries somewhere far from here. "What in hell's name are you talking about?"

The kid paused, placed a hand over his mouth in thought, then he tapped the gunwale wrapped in walrus hide and traced the outline of the boat in the air with twin forefingers. "How do you say this in Russian?"

"Say what? The boat?"

"Boat?"

Lukin made the same pantomime of the boat's outline, then pointed at the vessel. "Boat."

"Boat?"

"Boat."

The boatmen resumed their positions at the rails to launch. The kid grinned and set his hands to push on the bow.

"What are you doing?" Lukin demanded.

The kid pointed to his chest, then down into the boat, then jabbed a finger toward the ship.

"I think he wants to come with us," said Pamilan.

"Shit, why not." Lukin boosted himself up into the stern. "Alright, boys, push us off."

The boatmen heaved the craft into the water then jumped over the rails, splashing in their waterproof sealskin boots. The kid jumped onto a perch on his knees over the tip of the bow, then clambered down to sit up front as the men took up their oars and rowed toward the rougher water of the bay. He caught Lukin's eye at the tiller, then pointed at his chest again. "George Adams," he said, then pointed at Lukin. "How do you say in Russian?"

Lukin took a hand from the tiller and stuck a thumb at his own chest. "Captain Lukin."

Adams may not have spoken any Russian besides the single irritating question, but he did know what the Yankees on the beach needed first and what could wait. Back at the ship he clambered up the rope ladder with the ease of a monkey and disappeared onto the deck. When Lukin's men looked over at their captain he could offer them nothing more than a befuddled shrug. Up above there was a lot of arguing, then a load in a cargo net was swung over the side and Adams appeared once more. He came down the ladder as the load settled the boat down into the sea and the Russians opened the net and began stowing the boxes for the trip in to shore.

Adams pointed overboard at the water. "How do you say this in Russian?"

"Water," Lukin said, thrusting a crate into the kid's arms. He quickly stowed it and came back for another. They rowed away from the ship, raised their sail, and caught a scrap of wind that had picked up from the southwest.

Major Kennicott was waiting for them on the beach with a crowbar. Adams hopped over the side and started carrying crates to the pile of American gear. The Major prized off one lid, then the next, and evidently was pleased with what he saw. He clapped Adams on the shoulder, then turned to Lukin and the boat crew. Smiling, the Yankee commander held out a fist with his thumb pointed skyward.

Hakrin was standing in front of Lukin and twisted around with a frown. "That Yankee bidarshik just told us to sit our buttholes down on his thumb."

"He seems pleased with what we brought," Pamilan said. "I don't know why he'd insult us for it. Maybe it means something different to the Yankees."

* * *

That evening as he shuffled home in the slanted evening light, Lukin caught sight of two figures standing in his front yard. There was nothing so unusual in this, but as he drew closer he could see that Anastasia was talking to a man in a blue uniform. He quickened his pace.

Her eyes flicked over as he approached, and the man in blue turned to greet him.

"Hell's bells," Lukin said. "I should have known it would be you."

George Adams broke into a smile. "Good evening, Captain Lukin."

"Good evening. Do you need something?"

The young American's vocabulary had evidently grown during the day, but Lukin's reply brought only a furrowed brow.

Anastasia gestured at her father. "He asked if you need something, George. I'm sorry he's so grumpy."

Her words were no more comprehensible to him than Lukin's. He pursed his lips, then covered them with his palm, the same gesture Lukin had seen earlier that day. You could see his mind turning over in thought. Clearly the kid was no dunce, and given that

Hollister would be leaving with the ship, his initiative to learn some Russian was commendable. It was also clear that Anastasia found this hand-over-the-mouth gesture more than a little beguiling.

"Anastasia," Adams said to Lukin. "How do you say this in Russian?"

"She's my daughter," he replied in a level tone.

"She's my daughter," Adams repeated, smiling at her.

"No," said Lukin, "she's *my* daughter. Not yours." This irritated him far more than it should have. He pointed at his chest. "Anastasia is my daughter, not yours."

Adams considered this a moment. Anastasia was by now, despite what was proper for a well-brought-up Russian girl, hiding a smile behind her gloved hand. Lukin had often warned her about smiling too much around strangers but evidently there was no controlling her mouth around this boy.

"She is my?" Adams said.

Anastasia shook her head vigorously. "No. Daughter."

"What?"

"Papa, he wants to know how to say, *your daughter.*"

Adams' face brightened. He pointed again at Anastasia. "Your daughter?"

Lukin didn't know whether to be pleased at his little girl's sharp mind or dismayed at the rapport she seemed to have already built with this young American who no doubt had sex on his mind. In the dimness behind this thought lurked the notion that such a dismissive attitude toward youth was possibly a symptom of feeling old and used up, or perhaps the cause of it. Here was a chicken-or-the-egg question if ever there was one.

Adams grinned openly at Anastasia, and the way she blushed and ducked her head left Lukin feeling acutely old and irrelevant. Adams felt his stare and pointed rather quickly into the garden at the kale leaves. "How do you say this in Russian?"

"That's enough for today," Lukin said with a wave of his hand.

Adams' brows lifted under his forage cap.

Lukin hooked a thumb over his shoulder in the direction of the telegraph camp. "Get lost. We'll do more language study tomorrow."

"Ah," said Adams. He lifted his cap at Anastasia, then he put out a hand to Lukin. Lukin clasped it, briefly, mostly because it seemed to be the fastest way to get him to leave.

"Thank you help," the lad said.

"You're welcome. Now please be on your way."

Adams touched his cap brim once again, then turned and walked down the path across the tundra toward the white shapes of the tents. Over the distance, Lukin could see a crowd of curious locals hunkered around the Yankees' fires as they cooked their supper, watching their every move.

"Papa, why didn't you invite him to stay for supper?" She planted her hands on her hips and the gesture reminded him so much of her mother Natalia that his breath came up short.

"Because I've spent all damn day trying to figure out what Yankees are saying to me."

Anastasia let out a sharp sigh then turned and walked into the house.

"Don't you huff at me like that!"

She closed the door behind her. Not quite slamming it, but certainly not easing it into the jamb.

"You need to adjust your attitude, young lady!" His words hung lamely in the air. The telegraph camp was right in his line of sight; Adams had just joined the others and he could see Kennicott sitting on a drift log apart from the others, writing in a notebook over his knee. Frowning, Lukin looked back at the house. The light was fading from the day with the long night of winter following at its heels. *The September night is always immense after a summer of light*, he remembered from Anfisa and Yosif Denisov's wedding a few years back. His wet squishy feet suddenly seemed like not such a big thing.

2

SLOW DEPARTURE IN THE LONG DARK — CUCKOLD — BE A COWARD ON THE BERING SEA — VISITATION — THE BUTCHER ADDRESSES HIS MEN — ARRIVAL AT UNALAKLIT — THESE THINGS HAPPEN — A RUMOR — PLAN FOR INLAND RECONNAISSANCE — A TALK FROM THE BIDARSHIK — KETCHUM AND LEBARGE — A NEW LANGUAGE TO LEARN — UPRIVER FROM THE COAST — A PRIZE LOST — BIRD IN THE HAND — LEARNING THE ALPHABET — NOT A COSSACK — NOTHING TO SPARE — TAKE HEART

They sailed for Unalaklit in two boats on Saturday, October 2 by the Julian calendar, half of the Telegraph Men and some of their gear with the Russian boat crews. One vessel was captained by Lukin, the other by Stepanov. There had been high hopes for the steam launch and its hauling capabilities, but it had blown a valve on its maiden voyage and with no means for spare parts it ended up beached on the shore like a dead whale.

The morning was clear and decidedly frosty with everyone's breath rising in clouds to mingle with the mist rising from the flat-calm ocean. The haze of color on the southeast horizon foretold a big wind coming.

"You know these waters better than I do, Lukin," Stepanov said as they were making ready to depart. "I can manage a boat and crew, but I will need you to find the way."

"Very well." Lukin thought to offer to trade out one of Stepanov's crew for Pamilan, who had crossed the Bering Sea to Siberia at least a couple dozen times. But then he saw Iriana coming over to embrace the bidarshik and he turned away, trying not to dwell on the word *cuckold* and its myriad implications. *Let the son of a bitch manage the Bering Sea on his own if he can't keep up.* He stuffed his hands into the pockets of his peajeacket where his fingers touched the old blue bead. He'd found it trampled into the dirt several years ago at Nulato and it had ridden in his pocket ever since, mostly because he kept forgetting about it. He had a vague memory of transferring items from the pocket of his old worn-out jacket to this new one and finding the bead randomly stuffed into the folds of some old written-out list of things to do. But there always seemed to be some more pressing task than tossing the bead into the grass.

Iriana laughed at something Stepanov said close into her ear. Lukin fingered the bead, thinking, *Love like a bird flies away.*

The sled dogs howled from their pickets next to the palisade. Anastasia stood just down from the edge of the grass with a shawl wrapped over her head and pinned under her chin for warmth. They'd already said their goodbyes but he raised a hand in a final wave. She smiled a little, then he saw her eyes shift. George Adams was at the boat with the rest of the passengers, and it was obvious enough where she was looking. Lukin swiveled his head toward Adams who was smiling and just getting ready to blow a kiss when he saw Lukin watching. The youth gave a little start and made a show of bending over and digging in his pack for something.

Lukin shambled down to his crew with his hands back in his jacket pockets. "Are we ready to go?" Stepanov and his boatmen were already loading up their share of the Telegraph Men, Major Kennicott among them.

There were nods and mumblings, but nobody seemed very enthusiastic given the cold slow dawn that struggled over the horizon and seemed to be losing the fight.

"Fear not," Lukin said as he threw one leg over the rail, then the other. "You'll all be warm soon enough when you start rowing." He moved for the stern where the tiller was tilted up to keep it from dragging on the shallows. He pointed at the Yankees. "Into the boat with you."

They clambered over the side, finding whatever places they could among and atop the canvas-covered gear. Lukin waited until they were seated to his satisfaction. George Adams had made a point of sitting furthest abaft, closest to Lukin. He offered a greeting of raised eyebrows, but Lukin ignored him for the moment.

"Boatmen," he called, "Push us off."

Grunting like oxen, the crew shoved the boat out into the water and hopped aboard. Pamilan leapt onto the prow, then stepped down among the Yankees and made his way to his oar. From the top of the beach, Anastasia blew Lukin a kiss. Smiling, he reached into the air and pantomimed catching it and slapping it against his cheek. Only too late did he realize it had probably been meant for Adams.

"How do you say this in Russian?" Adams asked, pointing at the sail, furled around the stepped mast.

Lukin ignored him as the oarsmen started pulling.

* * *

The voyage north to Unalaklit was smooth at first, set to the pulsing rhythm of the oar strokes. But, as Lukin had expected, the wind began to rise in the forenoon. Sadly, it came from their port forequarter, which made moving under sail impractical. For a brief moment Lukin considered trying to get the canvas up and tack against the weather, but with the roughening sea and their boats so heavily loaded he reckoned they would actually make better time with the oars.

They pressed on with the bows throwing spray each time they slapped into a fresh wave. The Yankees donned oilskin slickers against the wind and sea. The Russians and Native laborers pulled on their kameliks made of sewn seal gut. Lukin had never liked wearing one, but there were plenty of times out here on the coast that you didn't want to be without it.

It was sometime in the early afternoon when the sea first came splashing over the gunwale as they plowed into a wave large enough to block their view of the horizon. A shout of alarm rose from the Yankees when they caught the full force. It was only a couple gallons, but it was a clear signal that it was time to let discretion be the better part of valor and point for shore. The oarsmen watched him as the water rolled down the bilge under the floorboards, then sloshed off the side as another dark wave piled up in front of them.

"Boatmen," he called over the wind, "bring her around to the starboard and get ready to stand the mast. We'll drive for the mouth of Fedorovia Creek to get out of this heavy sea." He put his fingers into his lips and let out a shrill whistle to Stepanov, perhaps twenty yards off. The bidarshik's figure at the tiller turned to face him. Lukin made the arm signal for turning into shore, for which Stepanov seemed all too glad.

The Americans did their best to stay out of the way as the oarsmen spun the boat around with its quarter-stern to the wind. Pamilan and Hakrin shipped their oars and unlashed the mast and stood it up, pushing it hard against the force of the wind. They pivoted out the spar and made the lines fast to the cleats bolted on the rails.

"Half sheet," Lukin ordered. The men kept the top corner of the spritsail folded down, and the wind filled the canvas in an instant. The remaining boatmen shipped their oars with obvious relief. Several of the Yankees appeared to be praying for deliverance. Two had their heads hung over the side, clearly green and seasick.

The mouth of Fedorovia Creek was just deep enough that they could squeeze the boats into the lagoon over the gravel bar with help from the incoming swell. Head-high waves pounded the outside beach cobbles as they made the boat fast with walrus hide lines. You could hear the head-sized rocks tumbling and clacking downhill each time the Bering Sea slid back down to rejoin itself, only to be picked up again and hurled onto the beach once more.

Inside the lagoon formed by the creek's tidal mouth, however, things were much calmer. "It's a damn shame to be wasting this daylight," Stepanov said to Lukin as they landed the boats on the lagoon next to a pile of driftwood.

"There's an old saying out here, Bidarshik," Lukin said, tossing a coil of line to Hakrin to tie off the stern. "A coward on the Bering Sea lives longer."

Pamilan found a roomy patch of dry sand beneath the sod where some previous storm had undercut the high bank and left the tundra mat draping down like a living carpet of crimson, white and amber. The Americans by this point were all shivering, even Adams. Some previous traveler had left a cache of dry firewood in the cave and Pamilan got a fire going at the downwind end to make tea. The hot liquid helped and everyone spread out their bedding and crawled into the organic cave. They huddled together for warmth as the storm raged and the rain flew. The roots of the plants tickled their ears and nose-tips like so many supple stalactites.

It wasn't an easy bed to sleep in and Lukin had been vexed with insomnia for many years, so it came as little surprise that he was wide awake as everybody else was drifting off. The boats' moorings creaked as the vessels rocked in the wind, which for a captain was not a sound to ignore. He listened for what seemed like hours in the gathering dusk, thinking about all the rainwater that would need to be bailed out. When he could stand it no longer, he crawled out and pulled on his kamelik. His feet squished in his wet moccasins and wool stockings but there was nothing to be done about that.

Inside his boat he was glad he'd come out to check because the water was up over the floorboards. There were sacks of flour and sugar in the cargo and nobody wanted those to get wet. Lukin found the birchbark bailing bucket and started scooping up water and dumping it out. He'd just flung the second bucketful over the side when he saw the figure pull itself up from the water and vault over so she was sitting on the rail. She hooked her bare heels onto the hide lashings inside the hull and planted her hands on the gunwale next to her thighs.

Lukin stopped, glancing back to the tundra cave where the others slept, then back at the visitor. "Zia."

Her hair was matted into a snarl of felty ropes that hung down her back and trailed into the shallows from where she'd come. Mussel shells and streamers of seaweed were studded into them. She wore not a stitch of clothing—in all the years she had followed him he'd never seen her in anything but her birthday suit.

"This is fine weather we're having," she said, flashing him a coquettish smile.

"Perhaps if you live naked in the cold sea." The posture of her thighs and the curve of her hips was distracting, despite the storm, as were her pink nipples and tawny skin. He'd first encountered her in a sandy cove near New Archangel when he was a student ditching his classes and she changed herself from a drift log into this form he knew best. Lukin was thirteen at the time and she'd seemed maybe a year or so older, the very font of pulsing intrigue for a pubescent lad. Yosif Denisov had found them just as Zia was about to drag him under the water in what she called "swimming lessons." Lukin could still remember the coho salmon in the stream flicking their tails against his bare legs.

School-age Denisov had flung a stick at her head and she'd hissed at him and changed into a river otter and swam away. Young Lukin had been left blinking and staring at the surface of the water where she'd disappeared, and as her visits continued through the years and across the shores and rivers of the colony as he'd gotten older, had children, become a widower, found gray hairs in his beard. Yet she remained in the form of a fourteen-year-old girl. And Denisov's warning to him still rattled in his ears: *She's somebody's cousin who drowned. She looks nice but she's a monster who wants to eat you and devour your soul so she can make you her husband. You'll never be warm again.*

"What are you thinking about?" she asked him from her perch on the gunwale.

"Things."

Zia lifted her eyebrows. "Yes. Things."

"Why are you here?"

"I wanted to give you another chance."

"Another chance." This was not the first time she'd said this. The rain freshened and drummed against his kamelik.

Zia seemed unfazed as the drops pelted her. She tilted her face skyward and closed her eyes, then looked over at him again. "There's something I want to show you."

Now Lukin closed his eyes. She often did this—showed him things on the surface of the water. They were things he'd grown weary of seeing, but there was a compulsion there, like picking at a scabbed-over mosquito bite, ripping it off to expose the raw flesh.

"Show me what?" he said with his eyes still shut tight.

"Look."

All around the surface of the lagoon was pocked with rain but next to the boat in the shelter created by the rake of the hull there was the slightest patch of smooth water. Leaning over, Lukin could just see the gray stones and bits of driftwood on the bottom and then somewhere in the water above it was the image of a man in an expensive-looking suit being escorted by a pair of naval officers and a detail of armed sailors down to a boat with its bow drawn into the gravel. Behind them a crowd of ragtag fur hunters followed. The town above—New Archangel, the capital of the colony with the logs walls of its buildings still fresh and bright—stood silent as the local Kolosh assembled in a line at the edge of the rainforest below the snowy mountains in their blankets and spruce-root hats.

The man turns and Lukin recognizes him instantly from the engraved portraits hung in his school classrooms. The high balding forehead and hawkish nose. Baranov. The colony's first governor. The Russian America Company's in-country manager. Later generations—Lukin's cohort of colony-born children with Native mothers—knew him simply as the Butcher. The man who had kidnapped entire families to force fathers and brothers into servitude to kill sea otters for pelts to sell in China, then routinely raped the mothers and daughters and encouraged his men to do the same. Their progeny became the colonial citizenry—Creoles like the Lukin family.

Baranov begins speaking to the assembled crowd. Do not believe the lies they tell you about me, he says to them. They will tell your children that I was a monster. That I burned and raped and killed and pillaged for my own ambition. They will teach your children in their school that I was evil, and they will try to convince you that I abandoned my duty to the Empire and sought my own profit at the expense of all else. But you know I have always worked tirelessly to do what was right for us all, to make sure we all had solid shares in this venture. Now the Czar has removed me and commanded my return to St. Petersburg and you all must go on here without me.

Many of the men weep, some with palms over their eyes, others with tears openly streaming down their faces. Most have not seen Russia for twenty years or more, and they have been followers of this man all that time. At the front of the crowd is a young man, dark hair, obviously a Creole from the shape of his face. Baranov himself is emotional—his voice wavers ever so slightly as he concludes his address—and when his words are done he pulls the young man into an embrace. Over the Butcher's shoulder Lukin recognizes this youth as his own father. The orphan Semyon Lukin whose parents were killed in a Kolosh raid and was later adopted by Baranov and raised in his house and would go on to become a faithful servant of the Company and a renowned fur trader and explorer. And as Baranov climbs into the boat that waits to take him to the ship anchored in Sitka Sound, Semyon Lukin, the mighty Semyon Lukin who would one day face down a rebellion at the fort he commanded with nothing but an axe and a musket, sinks to his knees and wraps his arms around his head as he convulses in sorrow. Baranov saved him from slavery among the Kolosh and replaced his father and now he is abandoned and alone in the world once more.

"Stop it," Ivan Lukin said to Zia.

"Stop what?" She hadn't moved from the rail. It was nearly full dark now.

"Stop it, god damn you!" he hissed into her face. "Baranov was removed because he was a murder and a violator of women. Your lies do not interest me."

She cocked her head at him ever so slightly. "I'm losing faith in you, Ivan."

"Then leave me alone. I have thought in the past that I wanted to rescue you from this prison you inhabit, but no longer. Leave me."

Zia regarded him for a long moment in the fading light. Mostly all he could see of her was her darkening shape. "As you wish, Captain Lukin." She rose, looked at him once more, then dove over the side. Her form slipped without sound into the lagoon and she was gone.

Lukin let out a long sigh and sank down onto one of the seats, shaking and unsettled and knowing there was no chance whatsoever now of sleep.

* * *

The trading station at Unalaklit was the furthest north outpost of the Russian America Company. Like most favorable sites for habitation along the Bering Sea coastline there was a sizable river that debouched into a tidal lagoon, with a long sandbar that separated the fort's waterfront from the open sea. They caught a good wind and made the run in a day and a bit with a stopover at the Golsovia River, but the name *Unalaklit* meant "windy place" in Malimiut and as usual the wind blowing down the river was contrary to where they wanted to go. Within sight of the fort the boats had to pull in the sails, step their masts, and come in with the oars.

The fort stood on the wide grassy sandbar with several dozen Malimiut houses built of sod over log frames. As with Fort St. Michael and Nulato there were houses and outbuildings, all notched together from drift logs and timber cut upriver and floated down to the beach. The place functioned mostly as a way station along the land and sea route between Nulato and St. Michael.

George Adams moved forward as they approached the waterfront to hop out and pull them to the beach. His instincts were good, but Lukin needed someone he could communicate with so he directed Hakrin up to the bow. The usual crowd was gathering at the beach and two Creole laborers helped Adams and Hakrin stall the boat's momentum and nose it gently onto the gravel. Stepanov put his boat into shore a few yards up the strand. Hakrin stood watching with a dour look on his face as Adams moved through the crowd, glad-handing the Creoles and Malimiut and asking them how to say this and that in Russian.

"Ivan."

Lukin turned from coming ass-first over the bow to see Ivan Denisov. "Yosif, I figured you'd be back at Nulato by now."

"I've been directed to wait for the freezeup and help you get over the mountains." He folded his arms loosely over his chest. "So these are the Telegraph Men we've heard so much of." The Yankees were doing their best to smile and be merry as everyone crowded around them, staring. They were the first Americans anybody had ever seen and all were curious about the exotic strangers from the faraway land of San Francisco.

"Such as they are," Lukin replied, shaking his old friend's hand and drawing him into a hug. The two of them had barely had a chance to talk when Denisov had been at St. Michael back in August.

"Those clothes aren't going to keep them very warm."

"I know it. My understanding is that we're supposed to get them outfitted. Somehow."

Denisov grunted. "They're definitely going to need better shoes. Those California boots will freeze their toes off."

"No kidding." The Yankees had been provided with tall leather boots with stacked heels and no room inside for anything but a light pair of socks.

Denisov frowned off to one side of his mouth. "This is going to become our problem at Nulato, isn't it?"

"Cheer up," Lukin said, patting his shoulder. "These things happen. And I brought rum."

* * *

As a married company officer, second in command at Nulato, Yosif Denisov was entitled to his own private quarters at Unalaklit. He pointed Lukin to a wide bench set beneath one of his windows, then dragged a chair over for himself. It was warm in the small room; the pitchka was going and you could hear the crackling and popping inside the stone firebox. Lukin settled down on the bench board and drew two bottles from his knapsack.

"One to share," he said, "and one for your own private use."

"Ah, very nice." Denisov had never learned to read properly, despite Lukin's tutelage when they were at school together in New Archangel, but he examined the woodcut image on the label of a sailor rolling a barrel onto a ship through a grove of coconut trees.

Denisov passed one of the bottles back to Lukin. "Set us up, would you?" He placed a pair of tin cups on the bench next to Lukin's thigh. Lukin tore the paper seal from the neck and pulled the cork. He poured a healthy measure into each cup and slid one to Denisov.

Denisov lifted his cup. "May we always have reason for a party."

"Indeed," said Lukin. They downed the drink together. Lukin reloaded their cups then corked the bottle and set it on the floor just inside the leg of the bench. "Any news of things at Nulato?"

"Same as always. We keep sending boats up the Kwifpak to buy furs at Nuklukayet and we get there after the Hudson Bay men have already come and gone. Your intelligence gathering mission the Company to Fort Youcon didn't seem to amount to much."

Lukin sighed. "I heard Sava took his retirement and moved back to the Gulf of Kenay."

"He did. He was pretty excited to go, too. Said he had a spot in mind for a house and a big garden where he could plant cabbages so the moose would come right up to his back door where he could shoot them."

Lukin grinned, feeling the glow of the liquor after a long cold trip in an open boat. "I'm all in favor of easy moose meat. How's married life?"

"It's good. Anfisa has more family than I know what to do with, that's for sure. And everybody seems to have something to say about her and that father of hers."

"Deryabin, you mean?"

"Mm."

Vasili Deryabin had been one of the founders of Fort Nulato, a man with a dark moody streak who had spent most of his career obsessed with finding and destroying the Hudson Bay Company fort built by the British on Russian soil. He'd been killed in an attack on Nulato and his only surviving child, Anfisa, was Denisov's wife.

"He cast a long shadow," said Lukin. "Are there any children on the way for you two?"

Denisov laughed. "No, but we keep trying."

"The fun is all in the trying."

"How's Iriana?"

"Don't ask." Lukin took a sip of rum. He thought to unload on his friend about her abandonment of the family, but he didn't feel like peeling back that onion right at the moment.

"How is it with your daughter home from New Archangel?"

"It's a mixed blessing. She's very excited about all this telegraph business."

Denisov stretched his legs out straight from the bench and leaned back. Lukin hoped he wouldn't get too drunk and obnoxious as the evening wore on.

"Do you think they can do it?" Lukin asked.

"Do what?"

"String the wire all that way."

"Maybe. Hell, who knows? It's a huge undertaking. Even just to maintain it, you know, finding and fixing breaks in the line. And then there will have to be some sort of treaty between the Czar and Queen Victoria and the United States. Seems like more of a headache than it's really worth."

"I hear you," Lukin mused. "I'm starting to wish the world would quit moving so damn fast." He took another sip and dug his pipe and tobacco tin out from his pack. "Stepanov says there are more Yankees coming next summer with the rest of the wire."

"Do any of them actually speak Russian?"

"No. There was a sailor on their transport ship who spoke a little, but he left with the boat."

Denisov snorted. "How in Christ's name are we supposed to help them if we cannot communicate with them?"

Lukin flattened his mouth into something that was not quite a frown. "That, my friend, is a very good question."

"God damn this fucking company."

"I'll drink to that." Lukin lifted his cup and Denisov joined him.

"But what would your old man say?" Denisov said when they'd drained off their cups.

"Probably that the Company's founders Aleksandr Baranov and Grigori Shelhikov were the greatest men who ever lived," Lukin said as he bent down to retrieve the bottle, "and we should be honored to be associated with their legacy."

"That sounds right." Denisov drew in a long breath then held out his cup for the refill. The neck of the bottle clinked against the rim as the liquor flowed. "Baranov was not much more than a hired thug."

"No argument from me. And thankfully, my old man isn't here to lecture us about his eminence."

They sat for a while, listening to the flames in the pitchka. Lukin thought for a moment to bring up the subject of Zia—they'd hardly ever spoken of her, and then only in the most circumspect of ways. But her visits and the visions she brought with them seemed to be getting more aggressive, as if she wanted to hurt him with them. Whatever she was, she had come from the country of the Kolosh and it had occurred to Lukin more than once over the years that being part Kolosh, Denisov might have some insight into how to deal with her. But every time he tried to broach the subject his old friend parried the conversation away. The closest he'd ever come to offering real help was a time about two years before when he'd said that it was taboo for him to speak of her, that only the most powerful of Kolosh shamans could discuss a creature like Zia in any detail. And St. Michael was about a thousand miles from the domain of the nearest Kolosh shaman.

"I heard an odd rumor from the sailing master on the supply ship this past summer," Denisov said.

"Oh?"

"He told me that Czar Aleksandr is thinking of selling the colony."

"Why would he do that?"

"The Company's been operating in the red for several years, Ivan."

Lukin was in fact aware of this but had not been overly concerned. He had his salary, and pensions were still being paid to retirees. And there was the prize money paid by the previous governor, a sack of gold rubles paid to him for the dangerous trip to Fort Youcon. This he kept hidden away in a series of secret spots. "But why sell it? There's still plenty of money to be made here. Any fool can see it."

"You know as well as I do how blind the Company's leadership is. And besides, it's just a rumor. There's probably nothing to it."

"Who would the buyer be, according to this sailing master?"

Out in the courtyard, not far from the room's one window, an English voice shouted something, presumably at the other expedition members.

Denisov lowered his voice. "The United States of America."

* * *

Right before Stepanov and the rest of the St. Michael crew departed the following day, he took Lukin aside. "I'm leaving Hakrin and Pamilan here at your service," he said.

"Thank you, Bidarshik." The wind was still whipping down the beach and it was hard to concentrate on anything else.

"The Yankee bidarshik, Kennicott." Stepanov gestured toward the old storage houses outside the picket that the local bidarshik had given them to fix up as their quarters. "He wants you to take that kid Adams up the river here to scout the route overland to Nulato. And to see about acquiring winter clothing."

"What do they need to scout?" Lukin asked with a frown. "Every man here has been over that trail at least a dozen times." The winter overland route to the River Kwifpak became something of a highway for dogsleds once the snow fell and everything froze over. It was hardly an unknown path into the forest.

Stepanov shrugged. "We are humoring them."

"I see," was all Lukin could manage.

Stepanov pursed his lips and folded his arms over his chest. "I want you to know that we're thinking seriously of resurrecting the push to get a fort built at Nuklukayet."

"Who is *we*?"

"Governor Maksutov and I. If this telegraph project is indeed completed, we will need to evict the Hudson Bay men and push our interests upriver. Maksutov is of the mind that getting rid of the British will happen with an international treaty. He also thinks you're the right man for the job when it comes time to move the trade upriver and build a fort there."

Lukin watched him, waiting for him to get to the point.

"So I'm going to suggest to you that it is very much in your interest to keep these Yankees as happy as you can. And also to fix your shitty attitude."

"We do all have our place in life." Lukin said flatly.

"This is true. So you will take Adams wherever he wants to go, and you will provide the expedition with every aid and courtesy. You will also provide me with regular reports on their movements. Is that clear?"

"It is."

"Good. And remember, you are a company officer, but I am not above having you flogged if you make me."

Lukin did not reply.

"Very good." Stepanov turned to head back to his boat.

"Take good care of my wife, Bidarshik."

He stopped and turned halfway back. "Oh don't worry, smart little Creole. I will."

* * *

Later that day, Lukin was drafted into service helping two of the Telegraph Men—Laberge and Ketchum by name—make the old storage sheds suitable for human habitation. The Unalaklit bidarshik had been keeping random paraphernalia there: dog harnesses and sledges in need of repair, empty barrels, old sail canvas and scraps of line, all the sort of extra discards from life on the far edge of the world, kept on hand for spare parts or for when some good use presented itself.

After they moved everything the main task was to pull up moss from the tundra and hammer it into the cracks between the logs with caulking chisels. There were only two of these, so Lukin used his axe to fashion one for himself out of a cut alder branch. These Yankees, he had observed, had an abundance of fancy tools and nifty gear, but it was all stuff they had to carried with them wherever they went. An expedient tool like his wooden chisel could be manufactured in a matter of minutes, used, and discarded. Such implements were much easier to carry in the head than on the back, as his mother had told him more than once.

Lukin stooped to gather another handful of moss from his bucket. Laberge was working next to him, up on a ladder nailed together from spruce poles. Using his fingertips together in a line, Lukin stuffed the moss loosely into the crack he was working on, then took up another handful. The idea was to spread it out and get it started, then go back over it with the chisel. When they had the whole building done they would smear clay over the outside of the moss to make it windproof, always a vital concern at Unalaklit.

"Hey," Laberge called down.

Lukin looked up. The man spoke no Russian beyond a few random terms he'd picked up since arriving, but he and Ketchum along with the others had worked up a sort of doggerel system of words, gestures, and pointing at things like small children that at least permitted the rudiments of communication. Even so, it was impossible not to notice how high-toned their speech was when they spoke to Creoles, how they kept their noses pointed ever so slightly upward. Ketchum said something in English that made Laberge smirk and Lukin didn't need to speak the language to see they were having fun at his expense while taking shelter behind his lack of comprehension.

Chuckling, Laberge pointed at the bucket of moss, then turned his own upside down to show that it was empty. Lukin waved the bucket down, then handed his own up. Laberge said something that Lukin had learned meant, "Thank you," then flashed that curious Yankee gesture of the fist with the thumb pointed up, delivered with a wide smile. Clearly it didn't mean *up yours* to them; it seemed to be a statement of approval. In any case, Lukin wasn't sure you could trust men who grinned like a bunch of donkeys at people they barely knew, but then it was obvious enough that as strangers in a strange land they were trying to be friendly. Already he'd observed Pamilan and the local Malimiut mimicking the thumb gesture to one another. He had even seen a local kid making the sign with his thumb pointed down at the ground while frowning and shaking his head. Evidently this showed disapproval while the upward thumb indicated the opposite. Even some of the Russian and Creole workers had picked it up.

Well, fuck it, Lukin thought, and pushed his thumb up at Laberge. Lurking behind this came the notion that if the United States was indeed getting ready to purchase Russian America, preposterous as such a thing might seem, it would be wise to acquire some English. If he could. When he was a small boy his mother had taken him to visit a giant who lived in a hole in the ground, and that large man had told Lukin he would always speak all the languages of the country. But Lukin had never made any progress with languages like Kolosh that were so far outside his country. He suspected the same would hold true with English. He'd picked up Koltsan—the language of the Kuskokwim headwaters—in his teens within a matter of days when he and his father started trading up at the Kuskokwim forks, and Yupiak as well when he returned to Fort Kolmakov after school. English, however, was just so much mushy-sounding blather.

He stole a glance up at Laberge. Who could imagine selling Russian America? He could recall learning in school that Napoleon had sold his North American holdings to the Yankees in 1803, so such a transaction was not without precedent, but who would give up such a valuable colony as this, a place that commanded the entire north Pacific?

* * *

Lukin and Adams left the following morning in a three-hatch bidarka with Pamilan in the bow. They were getting ready to launch when Adams spied the third paddle stowed next to his space inside the boat. He bent down and made to drag it out but Pamilan waved his hands vigorously. "Leave the paddling to us," he said in Russian.

Adams held up the paddle and pointed to it. "How do you say this in Russian?"

"Paddle," said Lukin, taking it from the kid's hand and sliding it back into place. "Now get in." He pointed at Adams, then into the center hatch.

Adams did as ordered, waving farewell to Kennicott and the other Telegraph Men on the beach, then said something that made the Yankees laugh.

The narrow bladelike boat made good time going upriver, even with just two paddlers. Not having much to do, their passenger busied himself trying to learn more Russian. All through the morning, he pointed at various objects and asked that same question, "How do you say this in Russian?" One by one, Lukin told him the words for sand, for rocks, for dead grass and grass still living. Riverbank, pan ice floating down with the current. Pamilan didn't say much. He already spoke good Russian and, as the bow man, had his hands full keeping them clear of rocks and drifting logs.

The hills in the distance crept closer. They entered the spruce timber that grew along the streams once you got away from the coast.

"How do you say this in English?" Lukin asked after telling Adams the Russian word for spruce tree. The lad quickly caught on to what "angleyski" meant in the question and spoke the English name. Lukin repeated it. They kept paddling.

It was late morning when they came around a bend and Pamilan paused his paddle to whisper their attention to a gray shape trotting toward them on the left bank. It didn't appear to have seen them.

Adams caught sight of it and pointed. "How do you say it?"

"Wolf," Lukin said, drawing his musket from alongside his leg. The wolf drew abreast of them, then stopped as if it had bumped into a wall. It stared at them while Pamilan worked his paddle to keep them even with the current as Lukin thumbed back his weapon's hammer and slipped a percussion cap over the nipple.

He had noticed in the back of his mind that Adams was digging around for something inside his hatch but was too preoccupied with watching the wolf and taking aim to pay much notice. Wolf pelts fetched a high price and the Company wanted every one they could get, so much so that they paid a twenty ruble bonus to any hunter who brought one in. And besides, wolves killed the caribou that everyone relied on for food.

The first shot from Adams' revolver took Lukin completely by surprise. He'd been taking up the slack in his own trigger but stopped as the bullet slapped into the dirt bank above the beach. Adams cocked the pistol for another shot as the wolf bolted for the trees. He fired again, missed, then cocked and fired a third time, wobbling the boat beamwise with each report. By then the beast was long gone.

"You stupid fucking kid!" Lukin shouted, barely resisting the urge to smack him hard across the ear. He only checked himself because dumping the bidarka into the river would have ruined everybody's day.

Adams twisted around and made an exaggerated shrug of apology. Pamilan kept the boat steady in the current as Lukin pulled the cap from his gun and slid the weapon back down next to his thigh. Adams was still looking at him when he thrust a finger square up into the American's nose. Both the smirk and the color drained from his face. "You do not touch your fucking gun in my boat," Lukin said. "Is that clear? You don't fucking paddle, you don't fucking shoot, you just sit there and don't move. You follow?" Had Adams been a company employee he would have pulled into the bank and flogged him a few stripes to drive the point home.

His tone was clear enough, even if the outburst was beyond Adams' linguistic ability. Chagrined, the youth slumped around to face the back of Pamilan's head.

Further upriver, with the sun as high in the southern sky as it was going to get for the day, Lukin called forward to Pamilan. "Your arms getting tired?"

"They are," Pamilan said.

"Let's find a place to eat lunch." Lukin paused his paddling long enough to flex his spine. Bidarkas were handy boats but they had the disadvantage that sitting in them with your legs stretched out straight ahead left your lower back stiff and sore after a few hours. You heard stories of the old-time Aleut hunters who used to routinely stay out at sea in their bidarkas for days at a time, but Lukin who had traveled in these boats since he was a baby had no idea how they could have done this and still been able to walk when they finally came in to shore.

They found some slack water on the downriver side of a wide gravel bar and nosed into the beach. When Adams twisted around to look at him, Lukin pantomimed exertive paddling, then panted like he'd just run a long sprint. "Time for a break."

"All right," Adams replied, which took Lukin by surprise as he couldn't recall the kid asking about that particular expression. Clearly he was paying attention to what they said between themselves.

They had just got out and pulled the boat onto the bank when there came the percussive sound of wings beating up from the alders and cottonwood saplings at the top edge of the sand. Pamilan and Lukin both knew it at once.

"Spruce hens," Lukin said to Adams in a low voice. Adams, thankfully, hadn't reached for his pistol. Lukin withdrew his musket from the boat, then reached into his shooting pouch for his leather bag of birdshot. Pamilan moved up and down on the springs of his knees, scanning the nearby spruce trees to find where they'd landed. He took a few steps upriver as Lukin dumped a handful of shot down over the lead ball already in the breech. Adams stood by, looking somewhat confused, but clearly smart enough to stay silent.

"There," said Pamilan, pointing into the upper part of a tree. Lukin rammed home a wadding to keep the shot in the barrel, then capped the nipple as he moved carefully to where Pamilan's eyes were aimed. All four birds watched them with a keen eye.

The cottonwoods had shed their leaves entirely, making a golden carpet that Lukin stepped carefully across. He paused, watched them. Their forms were slightly grayer than the spruce boughs in which they perched. They were all at the same level, more or less, and he saw that by moving forward a little he could line every one up in his sights. He took two steps, then a third, then raised the gun and fired.

Adams let out a cry of exultation as the four birds tumbled to the earth, flapping and clinging in vain as they fell. One tried to crawl into a squirrel hole and two more flopped to and fro on the yellow leaves. Pamilan snatched up these two and wrung their necks. Lukin pulled the hider from its hole, then scooped up the last one, stone dead from the lead ball that had torn its neck from its body.

"Grouse soup for the pot," Pamilan said, clapping Adams on the back.

* * *

They put in for the night at Lower Ulukuk, a summer fish camp that stood empty of both people and dogs.

"Everyone's gone to the winter village upriver," Pamilan said as they stood at the water's edge. There were about a dozen houses on the high bank above the river, with the usual ring of cache platforms built into the trees just beyond. To Lukin's mind, the lack of howling and barking dogs almost made the place seem even emptier than did the absence of people.

Pamilan waved a hand at Lukin's face. "Ivan?"

"Yes?"

"Do you care which one we sleep in?"

"I was thinking that one," he said, pointing. "The second from the right. It looks roomy enough but not too big to heat."

The summer houses were dug into the earth about knee deep, and the earthen perimeter inside lined with split logs in a vertical stack held in place by wooden stakes driven deep into the dirt floor. Above the earth, the walls were nothing more than sheets of birchbark held between the pairs of vertical poles that supported the roof. A central fire pit served for both cooking and heat, though the layer of frost crystals on the inside of the bark did not offer much encouragement with respect to the latter. They didn't even have a dog with them for extra warmth.

That night after supping on a stew of lentils, grouse, and black rusks, Adams produced a notebook and pencil. Lukin and Pamilan watched from the far side of the fire as the kid scribbled something onto the page. They all sat with their backs against the lower log walls, Lukin and Pamilan puffing on their pipes. Pamilan smoked his in the Malimiut manner, which was to put a large pinch of tobacco in the bowl, then get a flaming twig from the fire and draw the biggest draught of smoke he could manage, then hold it in until his eyeballs bulged out. Eventually he let it out with a smile at the light-headedness this produced.

The bark walls of the house, as was standard, had the white side of the rind turned in to better reflect the light. The fire's energy danced and flickered on the ceiling while the corners stayed hidden in the dim shadows. It was warm with the fire going but the thin walls offered no insulation and it was bound to be a chilly night. Pamilan finished his third bowl of tobacco, then lay back on the sleeping platform behind them, softly reciting to the ceiling a Malimiut love song. Behind them, in the hidden corners, voles and mice rustled about.

"Captain Lukin," Adams said.

Lukin had been mulling over what the sale of the colony might mean for all their lives, if indeed the rumor was actually true. It still seemed patently silly, but the nature of rumors was that you just never knew for certain. And nothing about it seemed to be good. It was widely known that in addition to their recent war over Negro slavery the Americans had been waging a hundred-year war against the Natives in the lands they claimed, and it was disturbing indeed to wonder what this might mean for him, his friends and family. None of this seemed to hold any promise for the future and the abyss of uncertainty stared right into his soul.

Glad for the distraction, he looked over to his left where Adams was holding out the notebook. He clamped his pipestem in his teeth and took the book for a better look in the firelight. On one side were written four characters of the Latin alphabet.

"You make Russian?" Adams asked.

Lukin frowned at the foreign letters, then extended his hand for the pencil. "Yes." He moistened the pencil's tip with his tongue, and on the opposite page wrote the thirty-seven characters of the Cyrillic alphabet. Adams scooted around closer to watch. When Lukin returned the book, Adams held it on his lap so they could both see it. Lukin reached over and laid some small spruce sticks onto the fire so it would blaze up and give more light.

Adams pointed to Lukin's A. "How do you say it?"

"Ah," Lukin said.

He pointed to Lukin's Б.

"Be."

He moved his finger down to the next letter, but needn't have done so. Lukin pointed with his left finger at the third letter, the В. "Ve," he said, then moved his finger down again to the Г. "Ge."

It was not lost on Lukin that having different alphabets made an extra hurdle for Russian and English speakers who wanted to learn each other's languages. But then here was an opportunity for him to learn the English alphabet as well.

He drew his finger down to the Д, but Adams held up a hand for him to wait. Taking the book and pencil he wrote beneath each Cyrillic character what Lukin assumed were phonetic pronunciations to mimic what he had spoken. Then he set the book back into position and returned to the Д.

Pamilan was snoring by the time they made it to the end of the list. Lukin took the pencil again and wrote his name: Иван Лукин. He pointed the butt end of the pencil at himself, saying "Ivan Lukin." Then, despite his interest in the lesson, he yawned.

Adams then started writing out words he had learned over the last several days, sounding them out with Lukin's help. He'd only made it halfway down the second page when Lukin, who like Pamilan, had been paddling upriver all day, fell asleep sitting upright. He woke with a gentle nudge from Adams, who shut the notebook and held it up, saying, "Thank you."

When he dragged himself outside for a piss, Lukin stared straight up at the dome of the starry night, thinking that he had only ever seen the stars for half his life, given that they disappeared for several months every April. He missed Anastasia. And Ilya and

Dmitri too. It was comforting to think of their innocent souls, both of them forever four years old, as stars in the sky looking down on him.

* * *

"Who is this Cossack?"

Valeria, the rather buxom young wife of the local chief named Amelkah, looked Adams up and down as they stood on the riverbank at Upper Ulukuk. Lukin had long since given up trying to explain to the local people that not every white man was a Cossack. Lukin always got the distinct impression they persisted in saying it because they knew it bothered Russians to be referred to as Cossacks. The Ulukuk folk were Deghitan, the same tribe as Lukin's mother, but their residence in such close proximity to the Malimiut people of the coast spurred them to adopt many of their words and cultural practices. Like the people downriver at Unalaklit, Valeria pronounced the word with a G, so that it sounded more like *Gossuck.*

"He's not a Cossack," Lukin told her and the others who had gathered. "He's a Yankee, from the United States of America."

"Where's that?" she said. Young children peeped out from behind their parents' legs.

"Far to the south." He pointed in the direction of the winter sun. "Adams here is from California."

California had once been part of Russian America, and the locals here at least had the vague notion that it was far to the south, though so far away that nobody could reckon the distance. The Deghitan knew a great deal about the geography of the colony's interior and the Kwifpak drainage, and even had a workable understanding of the Bering Sea, its islands, and the shores of eastern Siberia and Kamchatka. But the lay of the land in the wider world seemed a bit beyond them.

"There are more of them at Unalaklit and St. Michael," Lukin continued. It felt good to be speaking his mother's language again, even if these folk did have a thick accent, and squinted a bit at his Kuskokwim pronunciation and phrasing. In the back of his mind he wondered how to explain the concept of a telegraph.

"He looks funny," someone said.

"He does," Lukin agreed. "He's going to ask some questions through me. His boss sent him up here to see about buying some winter clothes, or maybe having some made."

"We don't really have anything to spare, Ivan," Valeria said gravely. "My husband and most of the men have gone up to the mountains to look for caribou tracks so we can maybe make parkas and boots for ourselves and our kids."

Lukin noticed that what winter clothing they had appeared to be left over from last year, patched and with much of the caribou hair falling out. "I thought that might be the case," he said. "But perhaps you could humor him."

* * *

They left the next day, empty handed. Heading down the Unalaklit River with the current they made it back to the fort in a single long day. The other Telegraph Men gathered around with Major Kennicott at the beach to congratulate Adams. All seemed to regard his minimal journey as a great triumph.

"At least you got to get out of here for a while," Denisov said as they stood off to the side, watching the scene of back slaps and congratulations in the gathering dusk.

Lukin frowned. "What a goddam waste of time."

"No clothing to be purchased, I take it?"

"None at all."

"Take heart," Denisov said. "I still have a half bottle of that rum."

3

FREEZEUP — OVERLAND TO THE KWIFPAK — DOGS FROM LONG AGO — KENNICOTT — DENISOV SEES THE MOON — MIRACLE AT LONE PEAK — THE BIDARSHIK IS NOT IN CHARGE — A HARD LESSON — USE THE WHIP, NOT THE AXE — LOOSE DOGS — THE TRAP IS SET — ARRIVAL AT NULATO — MASK OF ICE — INSTRUCTIONS — OUT OF THE SHADOWS — TWO ALONE — KURILA WITH A MOOSE — FITTING AND PROPER

The overland trail to Nulato froze hard by the start of November and Major Kennicott announced plans to move the bulk of his advance men and their outfit to the Kwifpak. Per his orders from the Company, Stepanov had been collecting all the extra sled dogs he could muster and shuttling them to Unalaklit along with dried fish to feed them. By the last week of October there were seventy-five dogs tethered outside the walls, making an enormous load of work for Yuri the dogmaster, to say nothing of their ceaseless cacophony of barks and howls. The Unalaklit bidarshik rallied the local Malimiut ladies of the settlement and, by means of generous offers of beads, needles, paint, scissors, and knives managed to purchase enough pairs of bespoke boots for the Yankees. Their feet, at least, wouldn't freeze.

They started inland on the last day of the month in a train of three sleds, moving up the trail with most of the Yankees walking ahead on snowshoes to break a trail down for the dogs. At Ulukuk, Kennicott hired several of Amelkah's men who had returned from a successful hunt to carry much of the expedition's baggage. Pamilan was needed back at the fort, so Lukin was left with Yuri and

Hakrin, and Denisov who with the frozen trail was finally able to return to Nulato. He switched off with Lukin piloting one of the sleds; Yuri and Hakrin drove the other two. The Deghitan porters moved right along the trail, but it was comical to watch most of the Americans who had never before walked on snowshoes. Laberge was the lone exception here—he seemed to have been born on them and could jog along to break trail with the best of the locals.

They camped at night under the stars with enormous fires, not for the romance of it but because there wasn't anywhere else to sleep. Dogs were staked out far enough apart that they couldn't fight over their food. Snowshoes and harnesses and empty sleds were hung up in the trees where the dogs couldn't reach them if they broke free. Loose dogs would chew up anything they could find and were particularly fond of rawhide lashings on sleds and snowshoes; these they would gnaw away until everything sprung apart and left their masters marooned in the forest.

Lukin was glad to have Yuri along. Koryak tribesmen were renowned as master dog drivers, and he certainly knew what he was doing when it came to their canine stock. He checked every single foot after feeding for cuts and sore spots. He pushed their lips aside to examine their teeth. The dogs seemed to know precisely what he wanted before he even laid his hands on them. They stood patiently as he examined them, something they almost never did for Lukin.

The first night out of Ulukuk, when they were sitting around their large fire, Yuri told Lukin and Denisov an old Koryak story about how dogs back in Kamchatka once had the ability to speak to humans. "This was long ago," he said as the smoke and steam swirled around them in the firelight. "A few families were floating downriver in canoes when some dogs on the bank saw them. Those dogs called out, Who are you? But the people didn't answer. They just ignored them and kept on going. This arrogance made the dogs angry."

"What did they do?" Lukin asked, poking a stick into the coals to get more air into them. A couple of the sled dogs tied up behind them raised up on their haunches and began to howl. It took only a moment for the others to join in. One of the Yankees at another fire yelled at them to shut up, a command that was entirely ignored. The amber firelight rippled under the spruce limbs overhead.

"The dogs called a grand council," Yuri continued, "and decided they would never again speak any words that men could understand. And they've kept that agreement all this time. But dogs are curious by nature, so they still bark at all strangers to ask them who they are and where they come from."

"You don't say."

Hakrin had been making ready to turn in for the night. Over the top of the licking flames he snorted and shook his head. "You believe that, Captain?"

"The world is full of mysteries."

Hakrin snorted again, then climbed into his robes for sleep. The dogs gradually settled down.

Quietly, Denisov said to Yuri and Lukin, "Now I will always wonder what they are saying to me."

Yuri nodded. "A good dog always has something to tell you." His face was youthful and bright in the long night.

* * *

The train of men and sleds climbed back out of the timber on the second afternoon, ascending the high pass between the drainages of the coast and the Kwifpak. By midday, rainbow spots appeared on either side of the sun, which forecast even colder weather on the way.

"The sun is putting his mittens on," Lukin said to Denisov when they stopped late in the afternoon to get a fire going with what sparse wood they could find, boil a kettle, and have a smoke. Both Adams and Major Kennicott joined them at their fire.

Denisov studied the Americans. "The Yankee bidarshik is having trouble," he said. Kennicott, with no Russian at his command, had no inkling of what was being said.

"I've seen him coughing like he was about to keel over," Lukin quietly agreed.

"He's been riding on my sled on the downhills," Yuri added.

Kennicott sat huddled up in his greatcoat, a woefully inadequate garment for the weather. He stared into the fire with his palms stretched out. His eyes had a sunken look to them. The Americans may have managed to acquire decent boots, but they still lacked parkas, mittens, and warm hats.

"He carries a heavy load of responsibility," Lukin said as he lit his pipe. "Being in charge of all these men and the entire operation. All while so far away from home." He puffed the tobacco into life as their kettle began to boil. Across the pass he could see the full moon pulling itself up from Heaven's floor and over the far line of peaks. He and Denisov had planned the trip to coincide with a full moon that would allow them to travel at night. This was standard practice, given the short daylight hours of winter but for Lukin it came with a price: A face in Kolosh iconography carved into the surface of the moon, a snarling mouth and two large eyes that had watched him from the sky ever since that first encounter with Zia so many years ago. When the moon waned down to a thumbnail there was still the one eye, peering down at him. Lukin had worked out over the years that this was Zia's true face and form. It was how she always knew where to find him.

He'd never told anybody about the moon, not even Denisov, but as they sipped their tea and the Yankees chattered among themselves he noticed his old friend staring at its face with unusual interest.

* * *

Lone Peak stood in the middle of the pass, rising up from the valley floor like a loaf of bread. It marked the entrance to the Interior. Some years prior there had been quite a commotion when Anatoli Rudinov and a crew of dog teamsters had been shown a vision of the Virgin Mary upon its southern slope. It had been February, the day after Holy Tuesday, with an immense aurora borealis casting the whole valley into a heavenly green hue. The teamsters had been traveling by moonlight but had stopped short at the sight of the Blessed Virgin shimmering against the mountain. According to Rudinov, they stood slack-jawed watching the image until the cold started seeping in through their parkas. Even the dogs had been silent, a rare thing indeed. But the image remained. Eventually the men dragged up some dead trees and built a fire to stay warm while they watched and prayed.

So many years later, Rudinov still choked up with tears pooling in his eyes when he told the story. According to his version, the image faded with the departure of the aurora and the men built a tripod of spruce poles topped with a crude Orthodox cross to mark the spot.

There were new caribou tracks in the area, and the morning after they passed Lone Peak Lukin agreed to let some of the Ulukuk porters go after them.

"Why did you let them go?" Denisov said as the hunters trotted down the valley on their snowshoes. The Telegraph Men were doubling up on their packs to carry the loads the hunters had dropped. Kennicott in particular seemed especially perturbed, but had been coughing too much to make an issue of it.

"Sometimes it's best to let them have their way," Lukin replied.

"They were hired to carry gear."

"So they were. But in my experience it's always better to let Native workers go off to hunt when they deem it necessary." There were any number of reasons for this, and with casual employees you wanted their help when it was needed, which meant you had to be flexible and stay in their good graces as much as was practical.

Denisov looked over at him, frowning.

"You don't approve, I take it."

"No."

"At Fort Kolmakov my father used to say that the bidarshik is not in charge of all this. First it is God, then the weather, then the Natives, then the Company, and finally you."

"We may all pay a heavy price for your old man's cheap advice," Denisov said.

Kennicott glanced down at his heavy pack, then went into a coughing fit as the porters disappeared into a dip in the valley floor. In all honesty, Lukin would have much rather gone with them. Up ahead, Hakrin stood by, watching as Yuri started his team moving with a whack from his long brass-tipped pole. He had to steer them around Hakrin who stood blowing on his cupped hands as Yuri and the Telegraph Men began moving down the trail.

"Hey!" Lukin called up to him, "Get your team going! I should not have to tell you this!"

Hakrin had been moving slower and slower since they left the coast, and this trend continued as they dropped down into the Kwifpak drainage. Toward the end of the day Denisov commented to Lukin as they traded off on the sled, "You're going to have to whip that Finlander like a plow horse to keep him working."

As it turned out, Kennicott saved him the trouble. Lukin had agreed to meet the Deghitan porters down in the timber at the forks of the creek that drained the east side of the pass. He would have preferred to go all the way down the Kwifpak before stopping, but he didn't want to get too far ahead of them. So they made a short day of it, the six Yankees carrying their double loads. That afternoon when they made camp, Hakrin's mood had gone from sour to outright surly. Kennicott had been riding on Lukin's sled for much of the downhill run, and his cough and color improved markedly, enough that he was able to help with the camp chores. After the dogs were unhitched and tethered, he handed Hakrin an armload of dog harnesses and, through Adams, asked him to hang them in the tree he was standing next to.

"Are your hands broken, Yankee?" Hakrin snarled. "Do it yourself. I don't take orders from you."

Kennicott's face turned stony at his tone, but Hakrin wasn't done. He waved a hand at the other Americans. "You are all a bunch of perfect fools to go to Nulato this time of year!" He stabbed a finger at Kennicott's chest. "You idiots can do what you like. I'm going back to Unalaklit. To hell with all of you!"

Lukin rose from where he'd been crouched to light the fire with his flint and steel. His dog whip hung coiled on a nearby tree. It was obvious that the moment had come to remind Hakrin of his place in the order of things.

The Major's voice was curt as he asked Adams what the Finlander had said. When he at last comprehended the nature of the situation he turned back to Hakrin, who wore an open sneer on his face like a scar. Lukin had just moved to collect his whip when Kennicott dumped the harnesses off his forearm, then leaned over and picked up an axe that had been hooked over the branch of a spruce tree.

"Don't hurt yourself, Major," Hakrin said.

Then, far quicker than Lukin would have credited, Kennicott flipped the axe around so he was holding it down near the head and struck Hakrin a sharp whack across the face. Hakrin saw it coming but didn't move fast enough. He went down but the Major didn't stop—he leapt onto him, getting a knee on his chest, swinging blow after blow at his head, shouting and cursing all the while as Hakrin mewled and wrapped his arms around his face and tried to twist away into the snow.

"Help me, Captain!" he cried. Lukin folded his arms and let Laberge pull the Major off him. Hakrin was by now curled up into a fetal position. Adams got a hand on the axe and gently removed it from Kennicott's grip. Panting in the cold, the Yankee bidarshik wiped the spittle away from his mouth. The dogs were all watching, as were the men.

Lukin moved so he was standing over Hakrin. "Get up and hang those harnesses."

Hakrin pushed himself to his knees and then to his feet. Blood ran down from his nose and his ear was cauliflowered. Clearly somewhat dizzy, he picked up his fur hat and set it on his head, then lifted the bunch of harnesses.

Kennicott watched him go, then spoke to Lukin.

"He says he's sorry for beating your man," Adams said.

"Do not worry over it," Lukin told him. "He had it coming." He held up his dogwhip. "But use this the next time you have to beat him. Or even just a stick. When you use an axe it's too easy to get in a hurry and hit him with the wrong end."

Lukin looked over at Hakrin, then raised a mirthless smirk. "He's lazy, but we won't get any work out of him at all if you bury the bit in his skull."

The porters came in just before dark with two caribou, having missed the whole affair. Denisov had no comment on any of it.

* * *

They made the Kwifpak two days later and stopped at the Deghitan village of Koltag to try and buy more fish for the dogs, and, not incidentally, to get out of the cold. The porters had cached most of their meat in platforms on the trail, so dog food was about to be a problem. Everyone spent the night inside a hot, stuffy Deghitan winter house. Lukin, Denisov, Hakrin, and Yuri supped on a fermented whitefish offered by their hosts, but the Yankees turned their noses up at it. The locals would not part with their dried salmon for any price.

The porters took their leave early in the morning, having only agreed to get the Americans to the river. In addition to not having any more dog food, the Telegraph Men could not find any men in Koltag willing to work as porters. Everyone was up and moving early, having fed out the last of their fish the previous evening.

"Where we sleep today night?" Adams asked Lukin as they were harnessing the dogs.

"There's a Denakeh fish camp upriver," Lukin said. "There might be some salmon cached there."

They traveled on the river now. Lukin got the impression the Yankees had been looking forward to a smooth road to Nulato and points beyond, rather than the jumbled mass of river ice they found. The icy wind screamed down the river's course like a monster from ancient myth. The expedition members were noticeably uncomfortable as it sliced right through their woolen greatcoats.

The fish camp above Koltag was abandoned for the season. When they pulled up in front of the summer houses, Lukin and Denisov snubbed their sled to a nearby tree so the dogs couldn't run away with it. They had to feel around in the snow with their mittens for the cache ladders where they had been laid flat on the ground, then clambered up the poles to the platforms.

"No fish," said Denisov, perched at the top of his ladder.

Lukin grunted. In the fading daylight he crawled up onto the platform and looked down at the houses of logs and birchbark, the men and dogs. The river and the forest beyond. "So the dogs will be hungry again tonight."

"We can make it tomorrow if we push hard. With luck." Denisov hadn't said very much to Lukin since the incident with the Ulukuk porters, and Lukin had been wondering if he'd given offense in some way. His old friend could be sensitive about the tiniest little things, and he suspected this had to do with never learning to read properly. He'd learned to mimic the diction of an educated man, but Lukin knew that writing in a book baffled him. Then again perhaps he was just sullen about there being no more rum.

"You doing alright, Yosif?" he asked.

Denisov glanced at him, then looked back down at the Americans. "Yes. I just want to get home." Muffled whistles sounded in the sky behind them. Lukin turned to see two ravens flying fast over the country to some destination he could only guess at; the whistling came from their wingbeats in the frigid heavy air. Beyond, the moon had shrunk down to three-quarters and hung low over the hills in the east. Lukin's eye traced the eyes and mouth carved into its face.

Denisov was studying the moon once again, with something close to rapture. Lukin was just about to ask him what he was looking at when Denisov shook his head ever so slightly and pointed with his heavy mitten back toward the coast. "There's the leading edge of the clouds. Looks like the cold air out here's going to keep that weather backed up on the other side of the mountains."

"Indeed." The darkening world slipped into shades of blue, white, and black-green, and Lukin wondered how to make life feel good again. There didn't seem to be much out there to work with. "Yosif?"

"Yes?"

Lukin kept his voice low. "What will we do if the Czar does indeed sell Russian America?"

Denisov slid his eyes out on the western sky, the direction of Siberia and Russia and China, all the lands Vitus Bering had spent years crossing just to get to the shore of the sea that bore his name so he could start building ships to explore what lay beyond. "Nobody knows. And certainly not me. But I tell you, Ivan, these men are not just here to string a telegraph wire." He looked over at Lukin from the corner of his eye. "I think it would be smart to get to know them well."

"They hold us in contempt. Because we're of mixed race. What are we to do with that?"

Denisov flattened his mouth. "So do most Russians."

"I doubt we'll still be giving orders to white men if the Americans take over."

"Think what you will. It's just a rumor."

Spoken like a man without any children to feed, Lukin said to himself. But as he climbed down the ladder he noticed Denisov watching the moon again, holding his head at an angle like a man who couldn't quite accept what he was seeing.

"Is there fish?" Adams asked when they came back to earth.

Lukin shook his head and looked to his team out of a nervous need to be doing something. Laberge asked a question.

"He wants to know if we must eat our fingernails," Adams said.

"What?"

"Things aren't that dire," said Denisov as he started untying the lashings on the loads in the sleds.

Adams clapped a palm to his face. "Our dogs, I mean. We eat dogs?"

Lukin looked over at Yuri and they both laughed. Even Denisov and Hakrin got a chuckle out of it.

"Those dogs are worth forty rubles apiece." Lukin said. "I've had to kill and eat a dog or two on the trail before, but trust me, we're not there yet."

All the same, their rations were down to a little bit of bacon and a few cups of flour, plus the remainder of the fermented fish, though Lukin doubted the Yankees would touch it. Inside one of the summer houses, with a fire going, he fried the bacon in a blackened steel skillet, then mixed some of the grease with the flour and water to make batter for blinis. These he fried in the remainder of the drippings while the kettle boiled for tea and the fermented fish thawed by the coals. The water had just come to a boil when Lukin heard shouting behind him. He turned on his knee just in time to see two loose dogs bolt to the hearth, nearly bowling him over. He was too busy trying to keep from toppling into the fire to pull the food away and this was all the time they needed. They gobbled the bacon and blinis then commenced fighting over who got to lick the pan. Lukin just barely managed to get out of the way as they rolled into the fire, scattering coals everywhere amid the stench of scorching fur, a rain of kicks and blows, and curses in Russian, English, and Koryak.

Laberge grabbed one of the dogs by the collar, which as any seasoned dog driver knew was not a smart move with the animal in a berserk fighting rage. The dog swiveled around in Laberge's grip and sank his teeth into the sleeve of his coat. Yuri clouted it across the face with his whip handle then deftly used it to pin the dog's neck to the floor so that its air was cut off, which settled it right down. Lukin did the same to the other dog using a stick of firewood. Only when the dogs stopped snapping and struggling did they yank them up by their collars and frogmarch them outside with their forelegs flailing uselessly in the air until they were tied up once more.

The fermented fish was the only food that survived the onslaught. Lukin rescued it from the ashes and Yuri rebuilt the fire. The Yankees, to a man, declined to partake.

"You'll be hungry, tired, and cold tomorrow if you don't eat," Denisov told them around a mouthful.

Lukin scooped up a piece of the redolent, cheeselike fish. "Those fools don't even know what hungry is."

* * *

They were only a mile or so out from Nulato with the dusk just coming on when they came upon Anatoli Rudinov and his daughter Sonia getting ready to set a fish trap into an enormous rectangular hole they'd cut in the ice. God may have afflicted Sonia with a simple mind and a harelip, but she was enormously strong and always willing to work. Moreover, Lukin had never seen her in anything but good spirits, something he'd always appreciated about her.

"Captain Lukin!" she called out in her doughy voice.

Lukin waved as the train stopped. Handshakes and introductions were made.

"What's wrong with the officer?" Rudinov asked Denisov. Major Kennicott had laid down on the ice when they stopped and was puffing for breath like a beached fish. Adams and Laberge hunkered next to him.

"He's taken sick," Denisov said. "He's been coughing and weak since we left Unalaklit."

"He told me he was getting dizzy spells today," Lukin added.

Rudinov's face was grim. "This is a difficult place to be ill." Several dozen whitefish and two large pike flopped listlessly on the wet ice where they'd been dumped from the trap. Their gyrations slowed considerably in the crackling cold as they froze alive, drowning in the ocean of air. Yuri's dogs made a lunge for them but he reefed back on the tugline and gave them several whacks with his whip handle.

"What's the food situation at Nulato?" Lukin asked.

"We got enough to eat. But that can always change."

Adams spoke from next to Kennicott. "Captain Lukin, can he tell us how far it is to Nulato?"

Rudinov, apparently unsurprised that one of the Americans could speak Russian, lowered his voice and leaned closer. "Does he not know you've all been over this trail a thousand times?"

Lukin rolled his eyes a little. "Go ahead and tell him. You're white, maybe they'll listen to you."

"It's just upriver," Rudinov said to Adams. "You can make it before dark if you hustle."

Lukin took a moment to help him and Sonia get the trap lowered into the water. Denisov stayed at the sled, watching, and Lukin felt a stab of annoyance that he didn't come to help, or at least send Hakrin or Yuri over. It would have been far less awkward and heavy with four pairs of hands instead of three. The Kwifpak ran full of mud and silt in the summer and clear in the winter under the ice, and it was only when the trap sank down out of sight that he saw her figure, floating in the water column with her long matted tresses waving in the current. She wasn't looking at him, but at Denisov as he leaned over from his sled, watching as if enraptured.

Neither Sonia or Rudinov had any inkling what he was looking at. Anyone watching would have figured he was just studying the lay of the trap.

Kennicott managed to climb onto his feet. Lukin stepped back from the trap hole as Rudinov and Sonia covered it with boards and shoveled snow over the whole thing to keep it from freezing up. He snaked out his dogwhip and gave it a pop to get the teams' attention. Denisov hadn't moved and Lukin had to snap his fingers at his ear to get his attention. They got the dogs moving, no small feat given the fresh fish that lay in front of them and Denisov's reluctance to move away from Zia's eyes and lovely figure.

* * *

The Nulato bidarshik Sergei Metrikov wasn't exactly overjoyed to see Lukin, but then Lukin hadn't expected him to be. They drove the dogs up the high bank and straight into the courtyard through the picket gate, shouting and cursing and slinging their whips. Doors opened and the usual crowd gathered to greet them.

"Safe journey, I trust," the bidarshik said to Denisov when things settled down. His whiskers were grayer and the pouches beneath his eyes more pronounced.

"Safe enough. We ran out of food for the dogs, though. These men here are with that telegraph expedition from the United States."

"He is their bidarshik?" Metrikov asked, looking over at Kennicott who leaned against Yuri's sled, bent at the waist with his hands planted on his knees. His uniform carried more gold braid than the others. Lukin stood at the stern of his sled as they ignored him.

"He is."

Metrikov lumbered over to the man and put out his hand. "I am Sergei Metrikov, commandant of this facility. I welcome you to Fort Nulato."

Lukin smirked, thinking that the old softcock could be downright cordial when it suited his purpose.

Adams translated for the Major, who straightened up and shook the bidarshik's hand. He looked like he might collapse at any moment. "Major Robert Kennicott of the Collins-Western Union Telegraph Expedition," was the kid's translation, though most of it actually came in English words.

"You all look cold," Metrikov said, clearing his throat. "Please, come inside with me." He turned away and coughed into his fist, then beckoned them to follow. Ice had collected on the men's beards and around the rims of their forage caps, frozen condensation from their breath and sweat. Metrikov led the way to his quarters where his wife Sabrina waited in the doorway wearing fine-looking Russian clothes. He stopped to cough again before closing the door behind them.

Footsteps crunched on the hardpack snow of the courtyard. Lukin felt the ice dangling from his beard like misshapen beads as he turned to look. Anfisa Denisova, formerly Anfisa Deryabina, had come out to greet her husband; she put her arms around him and Denisov bent down to kiss her. "My star," he said, smiling down at her. Lukin looked back down at his sled feeling a nonspecific disappointment.

"I've brought a guest," Denisov said, pointing over at Lukin.

Anfisa turned in his arms and her face lit up. "Captain Lukin! I didn't recognize you with all that ice on your face."

"That's easily forgiven, Madame Denisova. How have you been?"

"Lonesome." She lifted an eyebrow ever so slightly at him.

"Is Kurila around?" The lad had formerly rowed in Lukin's boat crew but he hadn't seen him for nearly a year.

"He's out hunting. Someone came in reporting moose tracks upriver. He's turned into the best hunter we have here, so Metrikov sent him out to see if he could get it."

"How long's he been gone?"

"Ten days or so. But you two should come inside for a drink of kvass."

"I'll take that deal," Denisov said, smiling at her again. He waved a mitten around at the three sleds. Hakrin and Yuri were waiting for instructions. "You can handle this, Ivan?"

Lukin looked at the sleds, then back at Denisov as he slipped his arm around Anfisa and turned her toward their quarters. His friend was in a command position here at Nulato, but it rankled Lukin to be ordered about in such a dismissive way, especially when he'd been in charge of the train since leaving Fort St. Michael.

"Of course."

"Come inside when you're done," Denisov said over his shoulder. "You're welcome to stay with us if you like."

He unloaded his sled with help from the fort crew, then marched each dog out to the dogyard where there were iron chains driven into the ground on wooden stakes for each animal. His team of five dogs settled down when he tossed them their fish, plus an extra half for each. "Go get warm and get something to eat," he directed Yuri and Hakrin. "Then feed them up for a day with hot broth and more fish."

"More traveling to come?" Yuri asked.

"Major Kennicott is heading back to the coast in a few days and we'll be going with him."

Yuri nodded and Hakrin looked sullen, which was no big surprise. Lukin went back into the courtyard and shook off his mitten and rapped on Denisov's door with the butt of his whip. It was full dark by this time, though the moonlight lit the way with its watching face, as ever. Denisov pulled the door open and beckoned him in as a cloud of condensation rolled inside. He'd doffed his parka but still wore his skin boots and waistcoat.

The amber lamplight showed the figure of Anfisa working to get supper together. She had cutlets made from minced grouse frying in a skillet and was just sliding a pan of cut potatoes back into the pitchka firebox after checking on their progress. Lukin closed the door and dumped his pack next to the wall. The room was warm from the cooking. He took off his hat, then slipped the dummycord for his mittens over his neck, then he pulled off his parka. This left him in his peajacket, vest, and shirt. He shed the jacket, then hung everything on the wooden pegs driven into the wall by the pitchka for this purpose.

Anfisa flipped the cutlets in the pan and wiped her hands on a floursack towel. She turned at the counter, saying, "Captain Lukin, please. Come out of the shadows."

Lukin had barely seen her in the past few years and was thinking of how she might react to him given that he'd saved her from being raped a few years back. Once at Fort Kolmakov when he was just back from school he'd seen his father beat a laborer to death with an axe handle for tampering with his own stepdaughter. The girl's Kitagmiut mother begged Semyon Lukin to stop and collapsed into shock when he broke open the back of the stepfather's skull with a final blow. The sudden memory left Lukin uncertain about how to act, but he stepped into the circle of light as requested.

"Semyon Lukin's son from Fort Kolmakov," she said.

"I see I can never escape my father's shadow." He put out his hand.

She laid a hand into his in a manner that struck Lukin as rather courtly and Russian, despite her uncovered hair. "I know the feeling."

There was a knock at the door behind them. Cold air rushed into the room when Denisov opened it.

"Kurila's back," a workman said. "He got that moose."

"Outstanding," Denisov said. "So everybody arrives all at once." He threw on his jacket and grabbed a pair of gloves. "I better get out there and get some of the meat before it all disappears."

"Bring Kurila with you when you come back," Anfisa called as he closed the door behind him.

Lukin watched the door for a moment, pulling the melting ice from his beard. He smiled. "So I guess I'm trapped here."

"Will you drink some tea?"

Lukin's cold cheeks felt puffy and itchy in the warm room and it was suddenly rather hard to keep his eyes from the waist of Anfisa's sarafan dress cinched in tight with a Canadian sash. A buzzing spread in his loins which in turn brought more flush to his cheeks. "I will. Thank you."

She stood a moment longer with her hands twisted into the towel, then lifted the kettle from atop the samovar and poured zavarka into a cup and set it on the table with a spoon. "Please, have a seat," she said, gesturing at the chairs and benches around their table.

He crossed to the table, watching from the side of his eye how the helix shadow of the loft ladder moved across her figure as she retrieved a jam crock from the cupboard next to the table. He took a chair, unsure of what to say.

"How was your trip in from the coast?" she asked as the water began to hiss.

"Cold," he said. "I'm still in a summertime mood. Winter seems to sneak up on me more and more each year and it takes a couple hours to get my gears turning smoothly for the day."

"The first trip over in November is always the hardest. Before the trails properly freeze down." This all seemed such a contrast to their first meeting that Lukin was left without his command of any language, a rare situation. Outside the dogs barked and yowled at the top of their lungs. The sound was sharp and clear through the log walls in the chill air outside. Now that he was alone in a room with Anfisa it was harder than he would have thought to pull his eyes away, though he was self-aware enough to think this may have been a by-product of his own marriage falling apart.

"Without a doubt," he finally managed as his hostess pulled the pan of potatoes from the firebox and set them on the stone top of the pitchka to stay warm. Lukin's stomach rumbled but he felt light and airy. "Madame Denisova—"

"Please, call me Anfisa."

"Anfisa, then. There's something I've wanted to ask you."

"What's that?"

"Do you recall what you said to me down by the river the night of your wedding?"

She shook her head.

"The September night is immense after a summer of light."

"Oh yes. I think I remember that."

"You were flying pretty high," Lukin said with a raised eyebrow.

She rolled her eyes. "It was my wedding reception."

"I've wondered if you read that somewhere or if you came up with it on your own."

"I can't read."

"Ah. Well anyway, it's a lovely line. I've probably thought about it every single day since then."

"Thank you." Anfisa seemed embarrassed by the complement. "There were several gifted song composers in my mother's family. Maybe some of that rubbed off on me."

The door opened and in came Denisov followed by Kurila. Lukin rose from the table as they both took off their gear, then embraced the youth. "Let me look at you, my boy," he said, stepping back. Kurila had grown so much that he had to look up to meet his eyes.

"Damn kid got tall," Denisov said.

"I'll say."

Denisov handed his wife a long moose backstrap, frozen hard as a stick of cordwood. "To be fried up for supper tomorrow."

Kurila took a seat on the table bench next to where Lukin had been sitting. "How have you been, Captain?"

"Getting older," Lukin said. And feeling my age. You'll understand in about thirty years."

"How far did you have to go to find this animal?" Anfisa asked Kurila as she set the meat on the counter with a hard clunk. She pulled out two more cups and poured zavarka as the kettle came to a boil.

Kurila rubbed his face. "Once I found the track, I trailed her three days on snowshoes." Moose were so scarce on the lower Kwifpak that a hunter who found a track would drop whatever he was doing to follow the animal day and night until he caught up to it.

"I've only seen one live moose since I left Kenay as a child," Denisov said. "I miss moose meat dearly living here at Nulato."

"That was one nice thing about living at Nowikaket," Anfisa said from the counter, "We had moose all the time there."

"Did you hear Captain Golinov retired?" Kurila asked Lukin.

"Sava, yes. He's back on the Gulf of Kenay."

Denisov eased himself back in his seat a little. "When I saw him going out at St. Michael he said he planned to raise fat cattle and cabbages the size of a washtub. Be a gentleman farmer."

"And eat moose meat at every meal," Anfisa said, nudging her husband as she set the kettle down on the table.

A disquieting emotion flared through Lukin. It took him a moment to recognize it as jealousy. He moved his eyes to the dark window. "I guess we'll see how he does."

"So these Yankees," Anfisa said. "They're going to string a telegraph wire between San Francisco and Moscow?"

"That's what they say. These fellows are the advance crew. They came in early to scout the route so they can start running wire next summer."

"Wouldn't it make more sense to just keep trying to run it under the Atlantic Ocean?"

"One would think. It's a hell of a big job to string a wire three-quarters of the way around the globe. And then to keep it maintained."

Anfisa seemed to doubt the prospects of this enterprise. She pursed her lips, raised her brows, but said nothing.

"These fellows came to run the wire upriver?" Kurila asked.

"I think only one of them is staying. His name is Adams. He's managed to learn a little Russian."

"How green is he?"

"Pretty green." He looked across the corner of the table at Kurila. "What do they have you doing this winter?"

Kurila shrugged. "Checking fish traps. Chopping firewood."

"Want to help drive dogs for me and Gospodin Adams?"

The lad turned his face over to Denisov.

"It's for Metrikov to say. But I have no problem with it."

Lukin stole the briefest of glances at Anfisa, thinking that she was likely just as handy with a dog team on the trail as Kurila. Her eyes flicked over to meet his, then dropped as she started refilling everyone's tea.

"Any chance you could talk to the old man for me?" Lukin asked Denisov. "He holds onto a grudge like it's money." Whatever the uppity mood Denisov had been in since Unalaklit, he hoped would evaporate now that he was home in the arms of such a beauty as Anfisa.

"I'll see what I can do," Denisov said, placing his hand over Anfisa's as she sat down again. For a moment it was almost like the rumor of the sale had never been whispered. The way she looked up at Lukin was quite proper.

4

A WORRIED MAN — OFF TO BUY SUPPLIES — NATURE'S AWE-INSPIRING SPECTACLE — VISIONS IN THE NIGHT SKY — READING THE TEMPERATURE — SURVIVORS OF CHIEF LARION'S ATTACK — SWAMPFISH — SETTING A BAD PRECEDENT — DISAPPOINTMENT — FATHERS AND THEIR CHILDREN — A CRISIS — STRENGTH AND COURAGE — ADAMS' TREPIDATION — THE FLAMES OF HELL — IN MEMORIAM — FETCHING THE COFFEE

Kennicott recovered quickly with a day's rest in the warmth of his assigned quarters at the fort, rooms that had once been Lukin and Iriana's. He and Laberge departed five days later, taking Hakrin and Yuri. The evening before his departure, he and Adams found Lukin while he was assessing the damage to a broken dogsled runner and how much time it would take to fix. Kennicott spoke at length and Adams translated as best he could.

"He want you stay here and work at me," Adams said.

Lukin had been down on one knee with his mittens off to probe the damage. He looked up from his work. "I have plans to spend Christmas with my daughter in St. Michael."

"Me sorry," Adams said with a shrug. "His orders are those. We must get warm clothes. And food. For when men come."

Kennicott, standing next to Adams, nodded solemnly.

Lukin rubbed his face to hide his disappointment. It seemed the cruelest of treatment to have your only child finally back in your life and then never be able to spend any time with her. And of course he was worried about her welfare. If she had enough firewood, or was running out of flour, or if the local workmen were sniffing around the door. Adams was by no means the only man who'd shown his interest.

Two days after the Americans departed, Lukin and Kurila took Adams upriver with a team of dogs pulling a light sled. Their first destination was a Denakeh winter village deep in the forest at the western foot of the Kaiyuh Hills, a place locally known as Ptarmigan Town for the abundance of those birds in the nearby uplands. Their route took them across the Kwifpak then over a dim trail through the forest, driving the dog team for two days and the first half of the night by the light of the waning moon. The path was faint and Lukin had to confess to himself he might well have lost it had Kurila not been with them.

The snow was also quite deep for that time of year, so Lukin had Adams and Kurila go ahead on snowshoes to break out a trail while he followed behind with the dogs and sled. The cold pressed into them from all directions and was made all the more intense by the shortness of the daylight hours. The breath of both men and dogs hung in the air behind them in a line like the exhaust of a steam train. The smoke from their campfires rose only thirty feet or so above their heads, then spread out laterally as if there were a glass ceiling between them and the night sky.

On the second night, sometime in the small hours, Adams shook Lukin and Kurila awake. "Look!" he said, pointing up at the sky. His eyes were wide with boyish delight.

Lukin had been awake for much of the night before drifting off into merciful sleep. He pushed his head out from his caribou skin sleeping robe into the cold. The fire was down the barest of coals glowing through the gray ash and the watching moon was waning down to half, yet the world was lit up by a pale green glow. He knew what it was even before he looked up.

"Aurora," Kurila mumbled, then rolled over onto his stomach.

Above them, shimmering ribbons of green fluttered across the heavens.

"It's beautiful!" Adams shouted, spreading his arms to the world.

Kurila started snoring. Lukin watched the green lights for a moment. When his nose started getting cold he pulled the caribou skin back over his face, thinking that Adams was going to be sleeping cold for the rest of the night—he'd risen without folding his skins and blanket back down to preserve the heat his body had left behind. Adams did eventually get his fill of the spectacle and crawled back into his cold robes, which left only Lukin awake to watch the skyshow as the dull headache built at the backs of his weary eyes. Against his better judgment, he started thinking of his grandparents, Old Ivan the Russian and his captive wife Ana from Kodiak. And Semyon. This he'd come to realize was how Zia got at his soul, how she nibbled away at the edges. Then Anfisa popped into his mind, the swell of her waist and the graceful way she moved around the house. He wasn't sure that this was any better, but at least it was pleasant.

The next morning, Adams showed Lukin and Kurila his mercury thermometer. It stood at -52 Fahrenheit, but the number meant nothing to either of them. Lukin only knew the Delisle scale used in the Russian Empire, and Kurila couldn't read. Kurila, always a bit impulsive, showed Adams the Native temperature scale by boiling a pot of water then slinging it out over the snow. It hit the frigid air with an audible *poof* and turned instantly to steam with none of it landing on the ground.

"It's fuckin cold," was his official temperature reading.

* * *

They traveled through the forest for two days and a bit, well away from the Kwifpak, then came to a broad treeless flat. The frozen trail cut straight across it, weaving in and out of large willows that stood hunched over under the load of snow they bore. Here they began to see the tracks of snowshoes and sleds. They stopped at the edge of the tall spruce timber to shovel away the snow and boil a kettle, sitting on their snowshoes around the edge while the fire melted the muskeg and cranberry vines beneath.

"The town is on the other side of this flat," Kurila said as they let the fire to blaze up. Far across, perhaps a mile or two in the distance, you could see the dark line of spruce and birch timber, with the domes of the Kaiyuh Hills beyond.

Lukin shook off his mitts and twisted them together on the dummycord behind his back. He stretched his palms out toward the flames. "You said you've been here before?"

"Metrikov sends me out here sometimes to buy meat and fish. Have you never been to Ptarmigan Town?"

"I've never been above Nulato in winter. These folks certainly picked an out-of-the-way spot to live."

"They're survivors of the Nulato fight," Kurila said.

Adams had been listening with his ear cocked. "Fight at Nulato?"

Lukin nodded as Kurila placed two thick spruce limbs atop the blaze, then set the kettle astride them, packed full of snow. He kept his eyes fixed on his work.

"About fourteen, fifteen years ago," Lukin said. "A chief named Larion came down from the Koyukuk River with forty armed men and attacked the fort, then he moved on to the Denakeh village next door." He paused a moment, watching the flames. "Kurila's parents were killed in the battle there."

"They come to kill Russians?"

"No," Lukin coughed then turned his head to spit out the phlegm. The dogs were hunkered down in their harnesses, watching the men. "It was a quarrel between Larion and a chief at Nulato. Deryabin and our countrymen just happened to be in the way."

Adams considered this. "I'm sorry at your parents," he said to Kurila.

"For your parents," Lukin corrected.

Kurila stared at the kettle as if it would boil faster under his gaze. He'd been a child of three, and had told Lukin once about seeing his mother falling to the ground, filled with arrows and still holding his hand. *There are too many awful memories in this world,* Lukin thought to himself. It made him dread summer when Zia would no doubt visit him again and show him more things he had no wish to see yet couldn't look away from.

Kurila cleared his throat. "Anyway, after that fight the survivors moved out here to keep away from Larion."

* * *

Ptarmigan Town's chief was a man named Tikungah. Kurila knew him well enough, but all he had to offer was a lump of frozen swampfish about the size of a man's head. Swampfish were nobody's idea of a delicacy—they looked something like an overgrown tadpole and were considered starvation food—but they were all that could be spared. But Tikungah sent one of his nephews with them to Ilya's Town, the next village up the trail. Lukin surmised correctly that Ilya was Chief Ilya, a name he'd heard associated with trading at the mouth of the Nowikaket.

For Lukin, there was a stab of grief at the name of his late son, and for some reason the memory of catching a frog with him in the muskeg and examining its iridescent eyes and little Ilya saying, "I wish my eyes looked like his." This had happened just two days before Denisov and Anfisa's wedding, right before he was stricken with the fever that took him away. Anfisa, however, was a much more pleasant thought. Moving along the trail on his snowshoes he wondered what she was doing at that very moment. He was brought up short by the notion that perhaps Ilya's death was God's punishment for his lustful thoughts about her. The whole mixture left him off balance and uncertain of how to feel about the world.

They spent the next two weeks making a wide loop through the country, hopping from one winter town to another. The locals seemed to have enough food to get along, which was good news for the fur business as it meant they would have time to set out traps, but like Tikungah's people they had little surplus to part with. Adams paid lavishly for what he could get with cloth, tobacco, and ammunition, though it ultimately amounted to not very much when viewed against the long winter. When Adams expressed disappointment at the paucity of the country, Kurila said, "Welcome to the Kwifpak District" in the dourest of tones.

They returned to Nulato with the swampfish, six whitefish, and a lump of bear meat for all their effort. Lukin noticed that Adams' mood had cooled considerably; he said virtually nothing the last two days of the trip as they drove downriver from the mouth of the Koyukuk.

"He's pretty down at the mouth," Kurila said to Lukin as they approached Nulato.

"Put yourself in his shoes. He's all alone here, with a big job to accomplish."

* * *

Lukin stayed once again in the Denisov house, sleeping in his robes next to the pitchka. Two nights after their return he was lying awake on his back, thinking of Anfisa, more specifically about unwinding that sash from her waist with her arms lifted over her head. There seemed to be nothing he could do to drive her from his mind. Metrikov had been a guest for dinner that night and between coughing fits he held forth about how undeserving Creoles were of the privileges afforded them by Czar. "It has been scientifically proven that people of mixed race are less intelligent than purebreds," he said, eating a forkful of salmon pie. "And besides, none of you Creoles would even exist if it wasn't for Russians like me. So tell me, why is it again that you pay no taxes to the Czar?"

You would think the man would keep this unique perspective to himself when sitting as a guest at another family's table, particularly a family of Creoles. But nobody ever accused Metrikov of being stingy with his opinions. And in the old man's mind it was in fact his table because he was the bidarshik and their house was under his domain. For his part, Lukin kept worrying that his own eyes were straying too much in Anfisa's direction.

There on the floor he prayed once more and forced himself to remember how after Dmitri's death Anastasia had taken to playing with the blocks he'd made for him. This was, as he recalled, about three years after the accident with Natalia, maybe a year after he and Iriana were married. It was winter, and her saint day was coming up, and seeing how much she loved building castles for her dolls he started sawing, sanding, and painting even more blocks for her to add to the set.

She was delighted with the present, sitting immediately on the floor and saying to her dolls that she was going to use the new blocks to build them a house like they'd heard about in the old fairy tales that Lukin often recited to her at bedtime. There were to be dashing princes with long fur-trimmed cloaks and shined boots, and real glass windows, and all the dried fish and caribou meat they could eat, with seal oil to dip it in. Lukin had been told those same old stories himself when he was little, right next to the old Dinneh ones, and he remembered smiling at his daughter with the warmest of glows as she laid this all out for her doll friends.

Semyon appeared in the memory, then in the last year of his life, coming in the door with a very large parcel wrapped in calico. "I'm sorry I'm late, my dear," he said to his granddaughter, "I was adding the finishing touches. He set the gift on the table—his knees were so painful by then that he couldn't bend them enough to set it on the floor where she sat. Anastasia climbed up onto a chair and sat on her own youthful knees so she could unwrap this new present. She was, naturally enough, bursting with five-year-old excitement. Her palms and arm had healed by then, leaving the puckered scars that she would soon start hiding with the long gloves.

"What is it, Grandpa?"

"Open it up and see."

Anastasia pulled away the colorful fabric to reveal an elaborate dollhouse. Two stories tall, Semyon had fashioned it from thumb-sized sticks in the manner of the log houses common to the country. He'd even squared the timbers with his jackknife and joined them at the corners with dovetails. There were doors and windows, a table, bed, and wardrobe, all made of tiny planks, with big cutouts in the long side walls so she could reach in to arrange the furnishings to her liking.

"I sized it to fit little Ludmila," Semyon said, pointing at her favorite doll. Iriana had made it from sealskin with human hair cut from her own head, and clothes of calico and rabbit skin tanned without the hair to resemble caribou leather.

Anastasia had been nothing short of delighted, and as a father Lukin was naturally pleased to see his child with something that would no doubt fire her imagination and keep her occupied. But as time passed it was hard to see the blocks he'd so carefully made for her collecting dust in the bottom of her toy box. "Kids grow up fast," Semyon had told him when he'd mentioned this a couple weeks later. "Before long she'll be too old to be playing with blocks anyway." It had been the closest Lukin had ever come to throwing his father out of his house. But then just before he'd departed for Unalaklit with the Telegraph Men he'd seen Anastasia using those blocks to build a miniature fort and town with Pamilan's five-year-old son who she'd been babysitting. So maybe things did even out in the long run.

"Ivan."

A hand was shaking him by the shoulder. Lukin opened his eyes to the dark of the room. Denisov was on one knee next to him, holding a candle.

"What is it?"

"It's Metrikov."

Lukin groaned. "Christ. What does he want?"

"He's dead."

Lukin cocked his head at Denisov, then saw clearly that he wasn't joking. He crawled from his blankets and yawned. "What time is it?"

"Seven a.m., give or take."

"By the stars or by the clock?"

"Stars."

Their footsteps squeaked on the hardpack snow and the sound filled the silent yard as Denisov led him across to Metrikov's quarters. Adams was wrapped up on a pallet by the pitchka next to the bidarshik's son and daughter. All were sound asleep but Lukin's ear caught the faint sound of someone crying. Denisov ushered him into the bedchamber. There was a candle on the shelf next to the bed and in the light he could see Sabrina Metrikova's hunched form with Anfisa sitting next to her, holding her.

Denisov set his own candle on the shelf next to Sabrina, then laid a comforting hand on her shoulder. Her cries were the most subdued of sobs, almost polite, as if she did not wish to bother anyone. Heartache flooded Lukin's soul for her and her newly fatherless children, not that Sergei Metrikov a grand model of fatherhood. He bent down to have a closer look at the bidarshik whose eyes were closed forcefully as if clamped down in pain at the very end. Anfisa drew Sabrina into another hug, and as her weight shifted the bed Lukin saw that Metrikov's body had already stiffened in death. He must have been gone some time before she woke to find him.

He walked around the bed and laid a hand on Sabrina's back. "I am sorry for your loss, Madame Metrikova. God has his plan for each of us." She could do nothing but wipe away palmfuls of tears. Anfisa was crying as well—he could see the candlelight glinting off the tracks across her cheeks. She sniffed and put a hand over her face, then drew Sabrina back to her and let her bury her face in the crook of her neck.

"I should tell Adams," Lukin said.

Denisov nodded. "I will be right back," he said to the ladies, then he followed Lukin into the main room.

"Who else knows?" Lukin asked in a low voice.

"Just you. And Anfisa."

Lukin looked over at Adams. His form rose and fell slightly with his sleeping breath. "Those children will wake up soon.

"I guess they will need to be told."

"I think they should hear it from their mother."

"I'm not sure she's up to it."

"They should not find out after everyone else in the fort knows. I can do it if you want, but it should not be one of those convicts in the bunkhouse who tells them."

"I will do it," Denisov said. "They know me much better than you."

"True enough." Lukin frowned at a crack in the floorboards at their feet. "You were his second, Ivan. So I guess you're the bidarshik now."

Denisov looked back at him. "I suppose I am."

In the back of Lukin's mind was a small but snarky voice saying, *So he gets to manage a fur post now. And you don't. And he cannot even read or write.* He recognized this as utterly selfish and shoved it aside for the time being.

"You wake Adams." Denisov said in a commanding voice. Lukin got the impression he'd been practicing it. "I'll talk to the children."

"Maybe we should have Anfisa bring her out here so she doesn't have to keep looking at him."

"Alright." Even in the dim candlelight Denisov could not hide that he was dreading this first task as the new bidarshik, but then who wouldn't? The man was dead and the lives of his children would never be the same.

Quietly, Denisov let himself back into the bedroom while Lukin padded over to Adams' pallet. He gave a muffled cry when he woke and said something in English. Lukin felt a sudden flash of irrational anger that he could not seem to learn enough of the language to even know what that syllable meant.

He put a finger to his lips as Adams sat up in his wool union suit then beckoned him over to the far side of the room where the children would be less likely to hear.

"Metrikov is dead," he whispered.

Adams had quickly stepped into his pants and was still holding them up with one hand. "What?"

"The bidarshik is dead. Denisov just came and woke me."

The Yankee rubbed his eyes a few times with the very tips of his index fingers, a wake-up habit Lukin had noticed on the trail.

"Just a minute," Adams said, then he picked up his night jar and turned to the wall. His urine splashed into the vessel as he emptied his bladder. Lukin watched the children, knowing they were likely to wake at any moment. Adams set the jar back on the floor and slipped his braces up over his shoulders.

Lukin beckoned him to follow and they entered Metrikov's chamber. Adams crossed to the bed. Some manner of realization seemed to pass over his face, but Lukin was too preoccupied to pay it much notice.

"Ivan," said Denisov from the doorway, "can you go to the bunkhouse and tell the men?"

"Yes," he said, though it seemed like the sort of thing that should be the bidarshik's duty.

"Sabrina," said Denisov.

She didn't look up.

"You should come out to the front room with us."

Sabrina choked out some inaudible Denakeh words.

"Pardon?"

"The children," Anfisa said in Russian. "She asked if the children have been told."

Denisov shook his head. "I will wake them for you."

She rose from the bed in a trance; Anfisa helped her to her feet. Out in the main room, Sabrina sank down onto a bench by the kitchen table. Lukin paused to give her a momentary hug before heading out the door. She stiffened a bit at his touch and it came to him that Metrikov had likely filled her head with all kinds of lies about him and the Creole Lukin family. He had certainly been that type. *Or maybe I just flatter myself thinking that I was that important to him.*

He moved for the front door but paused to offer his hand to the new bidarshik. "Strength and courage, Yosif. It's no fun to be in charge."

Denisov flattened his lips as they shook, a look almost condescending in its cast. "Don't I know it."

* * *

The moon was still up, casting its light over the courtyard. It was nearly full and the monster's face carved into it could be seen clearly, staring down at Lukin as he walked. Both Ursa Major and the dogs on their tethers were silent in the flinty cold and there was no hint of the dawn. He entered the bunkhouse. One end was divided into wooden stalls, not unlike a horse barn, so each man could have a modicum of privacy. The pitchka stood in the center, with the kitchen at the other end where the men did their own cooking. The whole place doubled as an indoor workspace when needed. Rudinov had his own house with Sonia but often came into the bunkhouse to take a cup of tea with his workmates before beginning the day's tasks. He and a man named Shabunin were up making blinis and tea while the other six men stirred about.

"Captain, good morning," said Rudinov.

"Good morning. Let's get everyone up. I have news that I only want to say once."

They set their mugs on the table and woke their comrades who hadn't yet put their feet on the floor. Lukin waited for every man to get his mug of tea.

"What is it, Captain?" Rudinov said when they had reassembled.

"Sergei Metrikov is dead. He passed away sometime in the night."

Kurila handed Lukin a mug of tea before finding a seat. Lukin cradled it in his hands as he leaned against the wooden countertop.

"Dead?" said Shabunin. He wasn't a convict but had formerly been a sailor and whaleman. Tattoos of a harpoon and knotted lines showed on his forearms below his rolled-up sleeves. Lukin recalled hearing some gossip that he'd joined the Company on a promise to put his whale-hunting skills to use in some new enterprise, but then he'd been assigned to Nulato. Not surprisingly he wasn't very happy about this.

"It's true. Madame Metrikova found him when she brought him his morning tea."

"So who is in charge now?" Kurila asked.

"Captain Denisov is the new bidarshik, at least in an acting capacity until we hear from the governor's office." The tea was hot but he gulped it down anyway. There was grumbling around the table.

"I don't take orders from Creoles," Shabunin said.

"You will follow all of the bidarshik's instructions with courtesy and respect," Lukin countered. "You would not be the first white man Yosif Denisov has had flogged."

Shabunin glanced sideways at his fellow workmen.

"That goes for the rest of you as well," Lukin said. "Most of you I do not know, so I will say this to you all. You may have some notion that it is against God's law for you as white men to follow orders from Creoles like Denisov and myself. If so, I will remind you that God is up in Heaven and the Czar is far away. And I can assure you that both imperial law and company policy are entirely on Denisov's side in this matter. Things will not go well for you if you defy him."

"What of his children?" Rudinov asked after a long silent moment.

"That remains to be seen." Lukin lifted his mug and took another sip. He had just set the cup back on the wooden countertop at his side when the door opened and Denisov came in followed by a roll of cold air.

"How is Sabrina?" Kurila asked.

"About like you'd expect. Anfisa and the Yankee are with her. Is there any tea left?"

Lukin looked over at Kurila who rose and retrieved a mug from the shelf and filled it for their new boss.

"You've all been informed about the situation, I take it?" Denisov said to his winter crew.

"We have," said Rudinov.

"Do we still have that stack of spruce lumber up in the warehouse rafters?"

"Yes, Bidarshik."

Despite the melancholy circumstance, Lukin noticed that his old school chum puffed up his chest at being addressed by his new title. He frowned ever so slightly into his teamug, thinking, *This is not a way to be in the world. Not at a moment like this.*

"He'll need a coffin," Denisov said. You and Kurila get what boards you need and start planing them down. Shabunin, I need you to find an old blanket and move Metrikov out from his bed. Put him in the warehouse for now. Captain Lukin and I will get his measurements."

Shabunin rose with the others. He rather pointedly did not look at either Lukin or Denisov.

* * *

The first gray light of the nine o'clock dawn spread over the fort and sifted through the bunkhouse windows when Kurila and Rudinov finished smoothing down the boards by lamplight. All the workmen gathered in the bunkhouse kitchen for their second breakfast. Denisov and Lukin joined them.

Rudinov and Kurila had set up their sawhorses next to the pitchka where the light was best. They set down their jackplanes, brushed the dust and shavings from their clothes, and sat with the others. Salt fish was passed around, along with dark bread, jam, and the rendered bear tallow that substituted for butter. Extra chairs and spruce stumps had been brought over as the bunkhouse came to serve as a makeshift funeral parlor.

"What do you think he died of, Captain?" Kurila asked Lukin as they ate.

Lukin shrugged, then looked across the table at Denisov. "I don't know. I haven't been around him very much lately. Was he ill?"

"I saw the Yankee give him some medicine yesterday," said one of the workmen whose name Lukin hadn't learned.

"What kind of medicine?" Denisov asked.

"I don't know. I just caught a glimpse of it as I was bringing firewood into the house."

Shabunin frowned. "Maybe the Yankee poisoned him. They're here as spies anyway."

"I doubt that." Lukin spooned some tallow over a slice of warm bread, then jam with a spoon. "He had no motive to do such a thing. It would be contrary to his mission out here."

Shabunin gave a derisive snort but held his tongue.

"There is plenty of talk that these Americans are here to cause trouble," Rudinov said.

"And it's just talk, Anatoli," Lukin said, chewing. "Don't try to milk your chickens."

"I barely know this Adams kid," Denisov said, "but he certainly doesn't strike me as a murderer. And Metrikov has been unwell for some time. You've all heard him coughing these last few months."

Lukin chewed another mouthful of bread and swallowed. "Adams is a good kid. He's young and too bold for his own good, but I've spent enough time with him to see the content of his character."

Rudinov raised an eyebrow. "Would you let him court your daughter, Captain?"

Lukin opened his mouth to reply but there came the clatter and thunk of the wooden doorlatch opening and closing. A moment later, George Adams stepped into the room.

"Speak of the Devil and he doth appear," Rudinov said in a low voice.

"That's a matter for some other time," Lukin said back. The fact that his daughter was of marriageable age was apparently no secret in the Nulato District.

Adams doffed his cap and balled it up in his hands. He cleared his throat. "Madame Metrikova wish time alone with children."

The Russians rose from their seats out of respect for the widow and her family. Chair legs scraped over the floor puncheons; knives and forks clunked on the table as they were laid down.

"That is well," Lukin said.

Adams' Russian words came out in fits and starts. "My friends. I am sorry for any harm I bring to bidarshik—"

Denisov cut him off with a wave of his hand. "Do not trouble yourself with this. God took him." He gestured to a vacant stool. "Come, please. Have some tea with us."

For a moment it seemed the lad might faint with relief. It was obvious enough that he was a long way from home, on foreign soil, and worried sick about the fact that the bidarshik had died right after he'd given him a spoonful of medicine. You couldn't blame him.

Later that day as the frigid sunlight began to envelop the world, Kurila and Rudinov kindled a large fire in the fort's cemetery to begin thawing the ground. They tended it through the night, with successive teams of workers periodically scraping away the coals to dig out the softened muddy earth, a few inches at a time. After each digging the coals were pushed back into the hole and more fuel was added to rebuild the blaze. Lukin had seen this done plenty of times for winter funerals but watching the process that night in the flickering amber glow he found it hard not to think of the flames as hell itself reaching up to claim Metrikov. Not a very godly thought, he had to admit.

When the grave was completed the following day, Lukin fulfilled his duty to God and the Company as a songleader by chanting the funeral liturgy and leading the service in prayer. In the deep cold the backdirt pile had frozen hard to the top of the ground adjacent to the grave, and they had to light another bonfire so they could finish the burial. Straightaway after the last shovelful was patted down, Denisov rolled out a barrel of kvass he'd discovered in Metrikov's kitchen—now his and Anfisa's kitchen—and the entire fort proceeded to get roaring drunk. In memoriam, naturally.

The new bidarshik was passed out and snoring sometime in the night when Anfisa sent Lukin into their storage pantry to get her some coffee so she could revive those revelers still on their feet. He took a candle with him and was peering around for the burlap sack she'd told him about when there was movement and she was inside the tiny space with him. A bonfire had been lit in the yard and they could hear the laughter of a story told in Adams' halting Russian.

"Here." Anfisa pointed and slid past him. The air between the shelves was so small that she had to move up against him and there was no mistaking the way she brushed her backside against his groin. Lukin felt himself swell and she caught his eye and smiled. She glanced out the pantry door then planted a rather girlish kiss on his lips. It was brief but sensual, and he was left too breathless and dumbstruck to think about anything else the rest of the night and for several more nights thereafter.

5

THE LIFE OF A TEAMSTER — LETTERS — THE AMERICANS MOVE INLAND — THE NUKLUKAYET PROJECT — STORIES OF TATHYALDIN — EASTER — FAMILY REUNION — A PROPOSITION — SAVORING THE RESURRECTION — TELEGRAPH OPERATIONS HERE AND THERE — INVITATION — GOSSIP AT KOLTAG — DUCK CAMP — SPRING CHORUS OF LOVE — VISITATION — COMMAND ME NOTHING — UNLOVELY THINKING — INTELLIGENCE AT NULATO — CONVERSATION WITH KENNICOTT — A SHIFTING

Lukin spent the rest of the winter of 1865 and 1866 going back and forth between Nulato and Koltag where the overland trail from Unalaklit came out onto the Kwifpak. The Telegraph Men had begun moving into the Interior in earnest and were staging gear and provisions, shuttling them in from the coast. Adams had been reassigned back to Fort St. Michael for the time being. Lukin hated to admit it, but he missed his company.

He didn't mind so much working as a teamster, and Denisov, now in charge of Nulato, let him take Kurila as his assistant. But every day was a slog when there seemed to be no future beyond the next trip up the trail in the cold. An acute loneliness for Anastasia gradually built into an enormous weight inside him. There were mornings in the winter's long darkness as the moonlight receded from the sky when it was all he could do to drag himself out of his sleeping robe, drink his tea, and get the dogs harnessed and lined out. The only thing that kept him eating was the knowledge that he would get cold if he didn't have food inside him.

The one grace note was that with so many men going back and forth from Nulato to Unalaklit and Fort St. Michael he was able to send and receive letters on a fairly regular basis. He had missed Christmas and Anastasia's saint day, though he did send her a present of two tanned fawn skins he purchased from an Deghitan lady at Koltag. The letters she wrote back tended to be on the generic side, with comings and goings of the company men and the Yankees, gossip from around the fort, and observations on the weather. He chided himself for being foolish enough to think that his nearly grown daughter would share her innermost thoughts with her father.

Letters from a loved one were of course wonderful but they were a pale substitute for a hug and a smile and the warm aromas of your own kitchen. When Lukin received one of Anastasia's letters at Koltag he would read it over and over by the light of the campfire, squinting through the smoke and the cloud of his own breath long after Kurila had turned in for the night. He always carried the new letters under his parka in the inside pocket of his peajacket, next to his heart.

When Lent began, he gave up tobacco as was his usual practice. It was unwise to swear off meat or fish or bread until Easter as this was generally all there was to eat. And being deprived of your pipe on the trail was certainly privation enough to focus one's thoughts on the sacrifice of the Savior.

Word had gotten around that the Yankees were buying all the provisions they could find. Folks from both the coast and the Interior started taking in extra fish and meat, then bringing it to the nearest fort to sell. A great deal of Lukin and Kurila's cargo was food for the Americans, and they got many a chuckle over the fact that Adams had paid so much for so little food earlier in the winter and now this openhandedness had set the prices that the locals were willing to accept, prices that were, by any measure, astronomical.

"Do you think they'll ever send you up to build that new fort at Nuklukayet?" Kurila asked him one night across their fire.

"Who the hell knows. I keep thinking I should move Anastasia in from the coast to make it clear I want the assignment. I even asked Denisov if he had any problem with me moving my household out here to Nulato." He missed his pipe and had nothing to do with his hands while the kettle hissed and popped. "But who knows."

"What did he tell you?"

"That he has no problem with me living at Nulato, but Stepanov has placed me at Kennicott's disposal so I need to clear it with him. You want to come up to work for me when it happens?"

Kurila tried to look disinterested. "I might."

Lukin chuckled. "Anyway, Denisov tells me he intends to push hard for the Nuklukayet project."

"Why are you so keen on the Tananah trade?" Kurila removed the simmering zavarka and poured it into their cups.

Lukin considered this while the lad poured in hot water, then added sugar. "I suppose maybe it feels like the sort of trading I know best. When I was your age down on the Kuskokwim, I would go up to the forks with my father in April to trade with the Koltsan. We took dog teams up the river, then built canoes and floated back down." He smiled a little wistfully into the fire. "It always felt like a little bit of a holiday. Especially when we made a big fur haul."

He accepted the cup that Kurila handed him and peeled off a little more dried fish. Kurila watched him.

"I suppose," Lukin said around a mouthful, "that maybe I just want to go back to the halcyon days of my youth. You'll understand that when you're older." He chewed some more and swallowed, then asked, "You heard anything of that shaman from the Tananah, Tathyaldin?"

Kurila shook his head. "Not much. Just rumors. Some Nowikaket men said they saw him and his hunters making big caribou kills up in the hills between there and the Tananah. I heard a wild story last summer that he killed a shaman from the Copper River in hand-to-hand combat. But he hasn't been coming down to Nuklukayet to trade."

"Where's he selling his furs?"

"Word is he's been taking them overland to the British at Fort Youcon during the winter."

Lukin looked up at the graven face of the moon where it hung behind the tall lines of the birch and cottonwood trees, peeking in at him. *Could Tathyaldin deal with Zia?* The man certainly wielded powerful magic, but first he had to find him, and he had no idea when he would get upriver again.

"Captain?" Kurila was staring into the fire.

"Yes?"

"Do you think the Czar is going to sell our country to the Yankees?"

* * *

He missed the Maslenitsa holiday that year but did manage to slip home to Fort St. Michael in late March with two weeks' leave to spend Easter with Anastasia. He traveled with a train of sleds and several of the Telegraph Men including Mike Laberge who by this point had acquired just enough Russian to get by. After nearly six months of daily contact with the English language, Lukin still could not make heads or tails of it, which was something close to maddening.

The vernal equinox was upon them and the days were long and sunny as they crossed Norton Sound and the jumbled blocks of sea ice forced up by pressure and tide. There was the usual gathering to meet their dog train and handshakes and greetings. The hardpack snow felt sticky under his Dinneh boots of tanned moosehide as he exited the picket, leaving for once the unloading of the sled and the care of the dogs to the workmen. *Perhaps I am indeed getting old,* he thought, but then Yosif Denisov wasn't there to boss him around and Stepanov didn't appear to care one way or the other, so why not take advantage of what rank he had.

Anastasia was walking in the lee of the house when he approached, hauling a pail of water. He could tell from the angle of her head that she'd heard him coming but she finished bringing the water inside and dumping it into the kitchen barrel before coming back out the door and closing it behind her. She wore black snow goggles carved from caribou hooves, as did everyone this time of year. It made it hard to see her thoughts.

"Papa," she said.

Lukin smiled, feeling his heart soar at the sight of her. He opened his arms. "Come here, Ermine."

She set the empty bucket in the snow in front of the door. Frowning a little she walked over and embraced him as he planted a kiss on her cheek. In his arms she felt both big and grown up and small and delicate all at the same time. It seemed utterly beyond belief that such a lovely creature could have come from him. There was a sudden urge to tickle her, make her giggle and squirm as he had done so often when she was little.

"Are you home?" she asked.

He pushed his goggles up onto his forehead and squinted against the blinding light off the snow. "Just for Easter. I have to be back up at Nulato before breakup."

Anastasia hugged him again. "George Adams is inside."

"Oh?" Apparently he was destined to see more of the overeager kid.

"He's helping us bake bread."

"Us?"

She lowered her voice to something just above a whisper. "Iriana's here too."

Lukin froze. Here was something he had not anticipated. "She's inside?"

"Yes. She showed up here drunk two days ago and won't leave. She says you two need to repair your marriage."

"So Stepanov finally got tired of her."

Anastasia shrugged. "She won't say."

He frowned and looked out at the sea ice, then back at his daughter. "I'm guessing Adams is not here to see me."

Anastasia's answer came in the form of a blush.

"At least he's learned some Russian."

She lowered her voice again and glanced at the door. "He's been spending time here so I don't have to be alone with her all day long."

A cloud of sunlight followed them inside the door. The house was warm and the iron plate that formed the pitchka door was nearly glowing. The heat wrapped around him as he stood blinking his eyes against the orange blobs left in his vision by the snowglare outside. There was the pleasant fug of rising bread. Iriana paused from mixing dough with a fork and came over to him. "Ivan," she said.

"Iriana."

She pulled him into an embrace that he returned in a perfunctory manner.

"It's lovely to have you home."

Is it, now? he thought. Over her shoulder he could see Adams at the counter with his sleeves rolled up and a lump of dough in his hands and a rather uncomfortable look on his face. Clearly they had not been expecting him, and of course when you'd been away for a long time you just never knew what you were walking into when you came through the door of your own house.

"Just for Easter," he said, looking back at Iriana.

"How was Nulato?" Her hands were sticky with bread dough and she avoided laying her palms directly on him.

"Cold and snowy."

"Gospodin Adams here has been kind enough to give us a hand with the chores." There was a bright eagerness in Iriana's eyes that Lukin found more than a little irritating. She seemed to think she could spend three years sleeping in other men's beds and then just come gliding in the door to have him back with open arms. The very thought of it made him want to laugh. He would have told her to get out right then and there but he didn't want to embarrass Anastasia in front of Adams by making a scene. And, he grudgingly admitted to himself, it was good to see the lad.

"Hello, Gospodin Adams," Lukin said. "How have you been?"

"Captain Lukin." He set the dough on the floured countertop and offered a dough-covered hand to shake.

Iriana stood by smiling as if this were a lovely domestic scene she had arranged herself. “Ivan,” she said, “why don’t you sit down. I’ll get you some tea, and we have kulitch.”

“What is kulitch?” Adams asked.

“It’s a sweet frosted bread,” Anastasia told him. “We save some of our white flour and sugar all year to make it. You might not get to try it again.”

Adams hesitated, then said to her, “I’m happy for stay if you like.”

“Please do,” she said.

Iriana seemed pleased for a chance to keep Lukin’s attention elsewhere. There was a long conversation coming, and the thought of it made him feel more weary than anything. The house felt awkward and off-level with her back in it, but hospitality compelled him toward geniality.

“I’m afraid you don’t have a choice,” Lukin said to Adams. “We’re not letting you leave.”

Iriana coughed a little, bending over slightly as she covered her mouth. She pointed to the countertop and Adams’ dough. “You have more kneading to do.”

Adams returned to the counter and started working the next ball of dough, and it occurred to Lukin that this must have been a Monday, as it was the common habit in the colony to bake the week’s bread on that day.

“Sit down, Papa,” said Anastasia, taking off her parka and tossing it over a bench against the wall. “I’ll get you your tea.” Lukin knew when to comply with orders.

"I'll be right back," Iriana said, throwing a shawl over her shoulders and head. From the doorway she said to Adams, "You're going too fast. And don't use so much flour! The supply ship isn't coming for another four months."

The moment she'd left he beckoned Anastasia back to the table. "Is she drunk?"

"Only on kvass."

"Has she been sleeping here?"

"Yes. In your bed in the loft."

Lukin scratched his beard and looked up at the ceiling. He noticed Adams listening with an ear cocked over his shoulder as he worked the dough.

"I have something I need to talk to you about," he said quietly. "But it will have to wait until we have a moment to ourselves, just you and me."

* * *

Easter had always been Lukin's favorite holiday, not the least because it came at the tail end of a long winter when sunlight returned to warm the world. By the Julian calendar the day of the holy resurrection arrived that year in the final week of March. Stepanov was no slouch when it came to celebration. The new bishop arrived at St. Michael the day before Good Friday. It was one of a scant handful of times Lukin could recall having a priest to perform the Easter mass. Usually it fell to him as one of the few trained songleaders in the region.

The end of Lent was eagerly anticipated by all, except perhaps the two Finlanders at the fort who were Lutherans and had to make do with their own prayers and devotion. Still, Stepanov as bidarshik would not see them excluded from the festivities, infidels or no. Nor for that matter were the Yankees.

Several of the families, including Lukin and Anastasia, went out onto the sea ice to spud holes for setting basket pots to catch king crab. It was the first chance they'd had to speak alone since Lukin had made it home; Iriana had been keeping very close to him and the more he stayed at arm's length the more smothering she became. He'd been sleeping downstairs next to the pitchka with Anastasia, despite his wife's entreaties to come up to the bed.

"So Papa," Anastasia said as they chipped away with their ice chisels.

He looked up at her. The world all around them was flat in shades of blue and white. Off to the north thirty fathoms or so were Pamilan and his wife and two boys working on their hole. Their dog team yowled at the empty sky and behind them you could hear the family laughing over something.

"What is this thing you wanted to talk to me about?"

"Yes," Lukin said. "We don't seem to get much time away from her, do we?"

"She is your wife."

"Mm, and your stepmother, such as she is. But I've been wondering if you would be interested in moving out to Nulato with me."

"Nulato?"

"The Company has been talking about sending me up to Nuklukayet to build a new trading station. I think it might be happening this summer or the next. But Nulato is where I would be based while we're preparing for the push upriver."

Anastasia stopped chipping and leaned on the long handle of her chisel with her chin propped over her hands. "And Iriana?"

"She will not be coming with us." Somewhere in the back of his mind was the image of Anfisa. There seemed to be danger all around her lovely figure.

His daughter watched him. He didn't have to ask her permission, but he very much preferred for such things to be done with common agreement if possible.

Lukin smiled a little. "And I have it on good authority that George Adams will be spending most of his time out at Nulato in the coming year."

She looked away, blushing again, but there was a smile.

"Do you really think I'm blind, Ermine?"

"I guess not."

"Look," he said, "I think this would be a good move for us."

"What will you say to Iriana?"

"I'm still working on that."

* * *

After Easter service the crab legs—some as big around as a man's wrist—were boiled in enormous cauldrons over fires in the courtyard. Stepanov had set a barrel of kvass to ferment on the first day of Lent. Everyone ate buckets of crabmeat broken out of the shell and dipped in seal oil, along with loaves of frosted kulitch and great racks of caribou ribs.

Lukin filled his pipe for the first time since Holy Tuesday and savored the joy of Easter as much as he could around the sour notes cast by Iriana. The resurrection seemed one of the very few things to feel happy about. There in the St. Michael courtyard with the fires going and the sounds of shells being cracked all around, Lukin poured himself another mug of kvass. Iriana was having an animated conversation with two Creole ladies. She paused to cough into her hand, then took a moment to catch her breath with the hand spread on her chest before continuing. He tuned his ear and caught the phrase, "It's always hard when they come back from the woods." Her words raised a nonspecific ire inside him; he'd been putting off telling her about his decision until after the celebration.

The band consisted of the Pole named Petroski with a violin and a Russian on a battered balalaika with worn-out strings. They played standing next to one of the fires where it was warm enough to sing and get decent sound from the instruments. Lukin watched George Adams lead Anastasia out to the crowd of dancers. He tried to show her some Yankee steps, which quickly had her giggling with her gloved hands clamped over her face. Mike Laberge and several of the other Americans started shouting and whooping while they danced the same jig. *These Yankees go around grinning like a bunch of monkeys, and now my daughter is doing it too,* he thought dourly. Adams spun her around and when he reeled her back in she gave him the thumbs-up, which set the lad to laughing so hard he almost lost the beat.

Iriana must have snuck up on him. He was startled to find her so close.

"Hi," she said, batting her eyelashes up at him.

"Hello."

"Anastasia is getting awfully familiar with that Adams boy."

"I have no problem with it. He's good company and he works hard."

She bounced a little on the balls of her feet, clearly feeling the rhythm of the music. "I've enjoyed being home with you."

Lukin sighed and set his cup on a nearby table. "My star, we need to have a talk."

"Yes." She cleared her throat.

He turned and led her away from the festivities to the relative quiet outside the fort picket. He opened his mouth to speak but she beat him to it.

"I have not been a very good wife, Ivan."

"Is that a fact."

"I haven't. I have been unfaithful." She looked down at her mittens. "For a long time. But I have been praying over what to do and God has told me to seek you out and confess, so that we may go back to living the way our vows require."

"As husband and wife, you mean."

"I do. You're going to need me up at Nuklukayet."

Lukin squinted at her. "What do you know about that?"

"Mikhail mentioned it."

"So now that Mikhail Stepanov has grown tired of you, and they're talking about making me a bidarshik again, you want to come back to our bed. After more than three years of adultery."

A small coughing fit overtook her and she buried her mouth into her elbow as if to hold it in. "I am genuinely sorry, Ivan," she said when it had passed.

"Was it the death of our son that made you look for comfort in another man's arms, or were you only interested in sleeping with the bull of the woods?"

"That's not fair."

"It is, actually. But I don't really care."

Iriana started to speak but he put his hand up for silence. "I am leaving you here. Anastasia and I are moving inland to Nulato so I can be ready to start the Nuklukayet project."

Her face drew into shock, then into a hard mask. "Just who do you think you are?"

"I'm your husband. And I am leaving you." He inclined his head toward their house where it stood on the slight rise above the beach, one of a half-dozen outside the picket. "You can have the house, and I will arrange for part of my salary to be paid to you." He felt a lightening as he spoke this, as if the turning earth might just buck him off into the heavens. "You are hereby freed of all your obligations to me as a married woman until we can arrange for a divorce."

Iriana appeared to have been struck speechless. She stuttered for a moment, finally saying, "It's Ivan Denisov's wife, isn't it? Deryabin's daughter."

"I beg your pardon?"

"Don't play dumb. People talk."

Lukin might have cared about her condemnation at some point in the past, but all he could feel was a distant detatchment. "Think what you like. I'm all done caring about your opinions."

"You're not half the man your father was," she spat.

Lukin laughed in spite of himself. *Only a fool has to have the last word,* he thought.

"We will be leaving the day after tomorrow. I'm sure you can find a place to sleep until then."

* * *

Lukin, Anastasia, and George Adams reached the Kwifpak in the last days of April, having detoured to Ulukuk for some unsuccessful caribou hunting. Anastasia had never been over the trail to Nulato and he enjoyed showing her the country—Lone Peak and the tripod with the cross where they stopped to recite a series of prayers for the future while Adams kept a fire going and smoked his pipe. April was a lovely time to be on the trail, with plenty of sunshine and the temperature cool enough to keep the snow in good condition for a dogsled. He couldn't recall having taken a trip such as this with her since before she'd left for school, and even if he did have to share her attention with Adams it was lovely to see how she took to the travel. She unhitched dogs and lit fires and piloted a sled at least as well as he did, and Lukin often had to suppress the prideful smile that danced on his lips when he saw how deftly she swung an axe. His sons had been taken from him but she was a joy to watch all the same. He didn't even mind it that much when she snuggled up next to Adams at night.

About half the Telegraph Men were assembled at Nulato when they arrived, making ready to start running wire up the Kwifpak toward Fort Youcon. Denisov had Lukin and Anastasia move back into the quarters he'd shared with Iriana all those years before. The room was full of memories that had soaked into the walls, but for the time being it was just a place to live until he could collect the timber to build a house. He had to leave the domestic setup to Anastasia, though, because Kennicott sent him right back down the trail to Koltag to retrieve piles of freight that had been staged there.

He had the briefest of moments alone with Anfisa when she came up to him as he and Kurila were hitching up two teams for the departure. He was worn out from all the travel and trying not to admit to himself that it wasn't quite as easy as it had been when he was in his twenties.

"I hear they're sending you back to Koltag," Anfisa said.

He looked up from the harnesses he was untangling. "Yes. If I can get there and back without having to build a boat. It's getting warm enough that I'm worried about the trail." Things were still freezing hard at night and there was plenty of snow, but the days had been warm and sunny and it was obvious that the snow wouldn't last.

"Your daughter is lovely." Anfisa didn't seem to know what to do with her hands. She smoothed her dress, then folded them in front of her, then finally settled on playing absently with a strand of her hair.

He smiled a little. "She is. She's a good hand in the woods too."

"Ivan Lukin, the proud papa."

He laughed a little, feeling the flush spread from his very center of him up his stomach and into his ears, to say nothing of the stirring in his trousers. "It's nice to be around you."

She met his eyes for a moment, then reached out and touched his arm. "I'm going out to look for ducks with some friends when it stops freezing at night." Out at the gate he could see Denisov approaching with Kennicott. Kurila was marching the next dog from its tether up to his sled's tugline.

"Stop by our camp," Anfisa said, composing herself. "We'll be downriver."

* * *

They made it up to Koltag without trouble, traveling at night when things were frozen and sleeping during the warmth of the day. Their cargo for the return trip consisted of wooden spools of telegraph wire that, thankfully, were of a size that would fit inside the sled baskets. There were also crates of what he would later learn were ceramic insulators for stringing the wire from the tops of the high poles.

They spent a night in one of the locals' winter houses, a large structure dug down into the earth with walls built of poles, birch-bark and sod. It was one thing to stay in one of these houses when it was empty, but quite another to be a guest in the communal life of the occupants. The place was hot and stuffy, full of the aroma of broiling beaver meat and the body smells of thirty-odd people crammed inside to hear what news the travelers had to share. Most everyone stripped off some or all their clothes, and it reminded Lukin not a little of the Deghitan houses of his childhood when his mother would take him to visit her family. Of sleeping in a pile of skins and blankets curled up with his cousins and the hunting dogs. Being dragged out of bed at first light by the old men and prodded with willow switches down to the river to make their daily swim in the frigid water. *You boys need to be tough*, was the old men's refrain, along with, *The first thing a hunter has to learn is to get up early!*

Lukin amused the small children by taking off his knit cap and pretending it was a diminutive lip-smacking monster that was all mouth and teeth and delighted at the prospect of chomping tender young flesh. A giggling child would reach out to touch it and Lukin would snap the mouth down over their hand with a loud chomping sound and the whole gaggle of them would scream and pull away, only to be back a moment later to test the beast again. These were the very last days of winter and it wouldn't be long before everyone moved into tents and smaller summer houses, because who wanted to be inside when it was sunny and warm after a long winter?

His ear caught two ladies talking about a woman at Nulato, saying she hadn't been able to give her second husband a child, just like she had failed her first husband. "Now she's been sleeping around trying to get pregnant," said one of them.

The other clucked her tongue. "You would expect more upright behavior from Deryabin's daughter."

"Girls bred from Russian fathers always have loose morals."

* * *

The temperature stopped freezing at night on the trip back to Nulato and the trails fell apart. Lukin and Kurila pushed hard, going without sleep to try and make the last run upriver in one go. Ice in the ponds back from the river was beginning to sink down into its own meltwater and the first songbirds could be heard among the trees. Thankfully, the river ice had yet to move. Waterfowl could be seen overhead in numbers. By the second day Lukin was starting to worry about the ice and began entertaining the notion that it might just be safer to stop and build a canoe now that the trail was turning into a linear mud pit with sketchy river crossings. The dogs were hot, surly, and hard to manage, especially when the frozen fish they'd been feeding them thawed and then started to smell. Their thick fur dropped away by the fistful in the warming world.

They were out on the ice of the main river when he heard the gunshots. Lukin braked his team. His two wheel dogs started snarling at one another. He shouted at them and they settled.

"Hunters," Kurila called from his sled over the barking and yowling of his team.

"Yes." Lukin squinted against the glare off the ice and the few white patches of snow that remained. "Anfisa told me she would be down here with Sonia and some others looking for ducks."

Two more shots cracked the air. Lukin had an idea Kurila was itching to get in some shooting himself. The kid was full of the boundless energy of youth and never seemed to tire, which was enviable for a man in his early forties.

"There's a slough that comes into the river around this bend," Kurila said, pointing up ahead. "That must be where they are. Bunch of ponds over there and a creek."

"Seems like you want to go look for some feathers." Now that they were stopped Lukin felt the fatigue overtake him. There as an enormous urge to just lay down in the melting snow and let the sun evaporate his body and soul.

"So do you."

Lukin chuckled. With Anfisa nearby he had something in mind other than wingshooting.

The hunting party was more or less where Kurila thought they would be, sitting in blinds made from grass and willow brush and paddling out across the open lakes to retrieve their birds in freshly built canoes. Their camp was at the main river just back in some cottonwood trees; the ladies and two kids came down to the bank as Lukin and Kurila pushed their dogs in from the main trail. Anfisa was the first person his eye found and the hug she gave him lasted just a fraction longer than the others. Her trim figure felt nothing short of heavenly pressed up against him, something he found both exciting and distressing all at once. The gossip he'd heard in

Koltag mattered not one bit and despite his worn-out condition he couldn't stop the buzz that ran from the confluence of his anatomy all over his skin to his fingertips.

"When did you sleep last?" she asked him.

He rubbed his face, wondering how long it would be before the dogs started fighting again. "We caught a few winks at Koltag."

"You two are staying the night," Anfisa said. "I won't take no for an answer."

"The trail's falling apart," Lukin mumbled. "We have to get to Nulato."

Sonia Rudinova and the children were already unhitching the dogs. Anfisa smiled. "You don't have a choice, I'm afraid. Besides, I can tell Kurila really wants to look for some feathers."

Lukin sighed, then pressed his lips together. "You certainly know how to be convincing." Somewhere in the backrooms of his mind he wondered if she'd heard about him and Iriana separating. Gossip moved both ways along the trail, after all.

"Come have some tea, you two," Anfisa said. "Sit by the fire."

Both Anfisa and Sonia had scarves tied over their hair in the Russian fashion, knotted beneath the chin. As Lukin shuffled to the fire behind Kurila, Anfisa withdrew hers and re-wrapped it around her neck so that her long braid trailed over her shoulder. She smiled again at him and he could see the faintest beginnings of crows' feet at the corners of her eyes.

Logs had been rolled up as backrests. The fire was built in the open space between two lean-tos fashioned of bark and sail-cloth, set so they faced one another. Lukin plopped himself down against a log, trying not to think about the fact that twenty years ago—even five years ago—he could have pushed on to Nulato without a second thought.

The hunters came back from the chase when Lukin was on his second pipe of the evening. They fed them roasted duck and rusks, with plenty of sugar in their tea.

"The Yankees are going upriver to the British fort this summer," Anfisa said as she cleaned up after the meal.

Lukin yawned. "I guess that means I'll be going with them." A fat lazy mosquito flew into his vision. He grabbed at it and missed.

The lean-tos were just big enough to accommodate the campers who had built them, so Anfisa and Sonia went into the forest and peeled sheets of birchbark. They fashioned them with some sticks and leather thong into an addition at one end. Kurila got up to help them, but Lukin had nodded off by the fire, still sitting upright with his cup of tea in his hand. Anfisa shook him awake when they'd finished putting down a makeshift mattress of cut spruce boughs. "I laid out your sleeping robe," she said.

Lukin looked behind her. His robe and blanket were indeed spread out over the boughs. "Thank you, Madame Denisova."

"You should really just call me Fisa, Ivan." Her hand still rested on his shoulder and she was close enough for her scent to fill his head. He wanted her more than air.

The others watched as he dragged himself to his feet. The dogs, tied to nearby trees, also watched with their ears up. They knew they were nearly done working for the season. "Good night, all," Lukin said. "Thank you for supper."

He didn't even remember crawling into his blankets but he must have fallen asleep because his Russian grandfather Old Ivan and his Koniag grandmother Ana were there. Their hut in the evergreen rainforest on Yakutat Bay, clustered with the others inside the picket of Fort New Russia. June month, the driest time of year, which means it only rains two-thirds of the time. But there has been a rare spell of sunny weather and the wheat the Russians and Cossacks sowed has started to put up the smallest of shoots. Yawning in the three a.m. light through the scraped sealskin windowpanes, Old Ivan rises from his pallet, steps over his sleeping son Semyon, and stretches. He has to piss and reaches for the doorlatch and is caught off-guard when the door is kicked in before him, nearly knocking him off his feet. A figure—humanoid, but with a grotesquely carved and painted wooden head—stands in the doorway. Iridescent hummingbird plumage flashes and its eyes of abalone shell seem a foot taller than he can credit. Old Ivan blinks at this creature's breastplate covered in a mail of Chinese coins as flames overtake the house across the way. More of these beings running across the courtyard behind him. There is a gunshot, then another, then two more. People shouting in Russian and Aleut. *Kolosh!* Old Ivan bellows, then the creature in the doorway brings the axe down square into his face, cleaving it open. Both the hut's windows are smashed in and more of the monsters clamber through. Ana is too startled to scream. Semyon bolts upright as one of the Kolosh drags his mother to her feet by a handful of hair and stabs a knife into her ribs. *Semyon!* she cried, reaching out. *Mama!* Then seven-year-old Semyon sees the musketshot that punches into her chest. The fire from the muzzle as sulfur smoke fills the room. He tries to reach for her but a hand grips his hair and yanks him back. *Mama!* but the one with the axe swings again and chops through the back of her neck with a single blow so that her head folds down against her chest, connected still by meat and windpipe as blood gouts and she blinks at him and at her own chest as she crumples to the floor. The flames. The whole settlement afire as Semyon is dragged by his hair down to the beach and roughly bound and shoved into one of the dozens of large canoes. The shouts of exultation. The severed Russian and Aleut heads hoisted on the tips of spears. Corpses dragged through the beachgrass and hacked to pieces with axes and daggers. The handful of mewling Creole children bound and whimpering for their parents against the damp cedar hulls as the canoes are launched into the water. Semyon Ivanovich Lukin, father of Ivan Lukin, is among them as they are taken deeper up the long, winding bay to their new life as slaves.

* * *

He woke sometime in the gray light of the wee hours to the sensation of warmth against him. At first he had the notion he was curled up around young Semyon in the Kolosh canoe, trying to comfort him as he would his own son.

There was breath against his nose. He opened his eyes to see the top of Anfisa's hair as she nibbled at his neck. He lay there, not moving, drawing a long breath and savoring the sensation of her lips in the tender area beneath his beard and the space between dreams and the world. Birdsong sounded all around from the forest.

She drew back and placed a finger to her lips. Lukin could hear the others snoring and breathing. She sat back on her knees. There was no scarf on her head and strands of tawny hair had pulled loose from her braid to trail provocatively around her face. Her hair had a little bit of wave in it, no doubt inherited from the Russian side of her family. Lukin propped himself on one elbow as a robin trilled its song from a nearby tree. *There's never any birdsong in these visions from Zia,* he thought.

Anfisa crooked a finger at him with a silent giggle. He hesitated for a single heartbeat, thinking somewhere that he needed sleep and she was married to his good friend and this was probably a very bad idea, then he crawled after her.

They walked through the trees to a stand of birch next to the slough. Pans of ice tilted from the shore into the tannin-stained water. Several of the birch trees had been recently peeled and bore wide bands of bright green underbark. Another robin sang from the forest just beyond sight. Anfisa watched his eyes as he stepped closer to her.

"What about Yosif?" Lukin said.

"The whole forest sings of love in the springtime."

"There you go again with the beautiful words."

She giggled up at him again and with one more step he was close enough for her to slip her arms over his shoulders. He kissed her and there was a momentary worry that he would have liked to have trimmed his beard first, but then conscious thought was pushed away as he set his palms on the swell of her hips. Her fingers trailed down to his vest buttons as he shrugged out of his jacket.

"I've wanted you like this for so long," he whispered.

She kissed him again and slid her hand down to his leather trousers. "I dream about making you hard," she whispered.

Somewhere in the slough the wood frogs began their chorus of spring love.

* * *

They were sneaking back toward the camp when Lukin spotted the figure standing on the ice, watching them through the trees. The moon had risen sometime in the remnants of night, bigger than he had ever seen it, as if it had come closer to earth just to peer at him through the trees with the one eye not hidden by the shadow of the earth.

"You go ahead," he said to Anfisa.

"What's wrong?"

"Nothing. But if anyone's awake it will look less suspect if we come to camp at different times from different directions."

She favored him with a sly look. "Sneaking around, are we?"

"We are both married."

Anfisa lifted his hand to her lips and kissed it. "The moon looks close tonight," she said, looking over his shoulder. Then she turned and moved quietly through the spruce timber. Back at the slough the figure had moved to shore and was standing next to a cottonwood where the water swelled around its knobby roots. Lukin walked back down to the water.

"Hello, Zia."

"Happy springtime, Ivan."

"Yes. How was your winter?"

"Winter means nothing to me. I see you've found a new distraction."

"I think I might actually be in love with her."

She said nothing, watching him.

"You sent me a vision tonight," he said.

"In your dreamworld. Yes."

"Why do you keep showing these things to me?"

"Because you want me to."

"Because you think it keeps me bound to you."

"Does it not?"

"What if I told you I no longer wish to see these things? I've already told you that, come to think of it."

Zia giggled and reached out to run a finger along his arm.

"There is a shaman who can help you," Lukin said. "He lives up the Tananah River." He recalled telling her back on the Bering Sea that he no longer cared to help her, but he supposed his good upbringing was getting the better of him.

"Whatever you want, Ivan." Her mouth hooked up a little on one side, as if humoring a small child.

"What is this force that keeps you enslaved?"

"There is no force," she said. "I am the force."

"Zia, the time has come for this to end." In the moment it dawned on Lukin how tired he was of her and their conversations that seemed to go nowhere at all.

"You're tired of me?" She cocked her head at him. Somewhere up near the watching moon a thrush let out its buzzing call, somewhere between a hum and a whistle. The Kolosh iconography graven into its face and thrown into the relief of shadows suddenly had Lukin's blood up. Perhaps it was the dream of the Kolosh killing his grandmother, or perhaps he was just weary of never seeing the moon as it had been before he met Zia so long ago in that cove near New Archangel.

"I'm tired of trying to help you all these years and just going around in circles. A long time ago my father set free a slave girl. He spent part of his childhood enslaved by the Kolosh, and when he became a bidarshik he used to buy slaves whenever he could to free them."

"That slave girl grew up to be your wife."

Lukin sighed. "Yes. Yes, she did."

Zia bounced up onto her toes. "You want me to be your wife?"

"No."

She frowned at him.

"What I want is to do the right thing. That which God's law compels me to do."

"You know I don't like it when you say that." There came a thrumming feel through the world as she spoke, as if the moon itself was pulling the earth and everything upon it toward its monstrous mouth. Lukin had only felt this once before, when Zia had tried to take him after Fort Youcon. It was like a wind, but far more viscous. The tree limbs swayed overhead. The open water of the pond began pushing toward the moon that now seemed even closer than before, bearing down upon him. Lukin's hair waved in the current like weeds in a stream.

"What are you doing?"

"You are not the only one who is tired of being played with, Ivan. You have a choice to make."

"You want my soul, not me. Don't pretend it's anything else."

She walked a circle around him. "You want to give your soul to the wife of that friend of yours. The one who caught us all those years ago back at the cove."

"Yosif Denisov," he said and realized too late the mistake he'd made. Now she knew his name. And that meant she had the opening she needed for him.

"Yosif Denisov," she said, turning the syllables over in her mouth. Lukin turned to keep facing her, or more specifically to avoid turning his back to her.

"You've already given your soul to her. I see it now, Ivan."

"I have given a piece of myself to her," Lukin admitted. "But it's a piece of my heart. My soul belongs to God and to my country."

"Yosif Denisov," she repeated, still scoring her circle. Her matted hair had grown more wild, and her teeth seemed longer, more fanglike. Without any warning she darted in at him and hissed, clacking her teeth together as she flashed a taunting smile that looked very much like the one the moon wore.

Lukin stood his ground. "This shaman on the Tananah has powerful magic. The most powerful I've ever encountered. We can set you free so that you no longer crave the souls of others." He was careful not to speak Tathyaldin's name.

"You will get rid of her," Zia said. "I'm giving you this one last chance."

Her voice sounded like the grinding of ice cakes in the spring breakup.

"Get rid of who?" His pulse hammered in his ears.

"Her. Denisov's wife." She glared at him from under her brows.

"I'm not going to do that."

Her eyes had turned solid black, the whites and irises gone as if they never were. "If you don't, I will take him."

"That would be unwise, Zia."

"*I said get rid of her!*"

Lukin drew the voluted dagger from beneath his vest. "*I am Captain Ivan Semyonovich Lukin and you command me nothing!*" The birdsong had halted and his voice filled the forest and sky. Zia screeched as he came at her and he would not have credited how fast the change happened. The creature she became was something like a river otter the size of a wolf but with the head and spines and gaping mouth of a sculpin. The sort of thing that could gulp both your soul and your body together in one go. She lunged at him and he drove the dagger into her throat under her chin. She twisted away, swiping at him with her claws and he pulled the steel out and slashed it at her as she came again, bowling him hard enough against a cottonwood tree to knock his breath away. The blade sliced one of her spines clean off. She made another lunge at him with her mouth and he stepped back to get her in close and drove the dagger in again. The current pulling them toward the moon was now so intense it threatened his balance. The world hummed around them and the moon's eye blinked like an aspen leaf falling to the ground as its mouth opened still wider.

Lukin sucked in a breath against the wind. "*Get out of my country!*" Zia chomped at him, spinning around. He charged her once more and she plunged into the pond. There was the dim form of her swimming, stroking wide under the water with her arms with her hair trailing behind her, then she was gone. The thrumming current dimmed, then faded away. When Lukin looked up at the moon it hung once again at its normal distance. But the eye still watched him. And when he looked around, panting with the chilly sweat soaking his shirt, there next to the cottonwood roots was a lock of matted black hair with mussel shells and spruce needles felted into it.

* * *

The dogs at Nulato sent up their normal howling as Lukin and Kurila pulled into the gate the next morning pushing and dragging their heavy sleds over the very last remnants of the snow. Anatoli Rudinov was the only one who came out to greet them.

"Everyone's out chasing duck feathers?" Kurila asked.

"Yes. Did you see Sonia and Anfisa downriver?"

Lukin managed not to hesitate. He'd spent the day dwelling on the old maxim of the colony that a man took a Russian wife to have her to himself, or a Creole wife to share her with every man in town. It was an unlovely thought at the best of times and his mind felt off balance from his encounter with Zia and what it meant for the future. "We did. They're getting along well. They had lots of ducks and geese being smoked and salted down."

"That's good. I love those first smoked ducks in the spring." He studied the rotten river ice, then regarded Lukin with a look he couldn't quite parse. "Did you hear that Denisov has taken Sabrina Metrikova as a second wife?" Polygamous marriages were not uncommon in the hinterlands of Russian America, a cultural influence from the Native societies. The Orthodox clergy condemned it for obvious reasons, but with their influence spread so thin over such a vast area there wasn't much they could do.

"Is this some shitty bunkhouse gossip?"

Rudinov shook his head. "It's true. Sabrina is the lady of his house now."

"I'm guessing Anfisa is not very pleased about this."

"She's moving out to live with her Native relations. I heard she told Denisov that she would not accept a second wife in their house."

Lukin couldn't think of a single thing to say in response to this.

"Are you alright, Captain?"

"Yes. What about Metrikov's children?"

"Captain Denisov took them in as his stepchildren. The Company refused to support them as orphans." He smirked at Lukin. "From the sound of things, he and Sabrina are trying hard for more."

Lukin arched an eyebrow at him, wondering why Anfisa had said nothing about this development in her life. Perhaps she was indeed trying to get a baby inside her to win back Denisov's affections, though with all the hearsay flying around this seemed an especially reckless course of action, and she'd never struck him as the reckless type.

He looked around the courtyard as Kurila began unhitching the teams. "Where is my daughter?"

"She and some of the ladies went out in the woods peeling birchbark for a couple days. I'm the only one here at the moment besides the Yankees."

"Lukin." It was Frank Ketchum, flanked by Mike Laberge and Major Kennicott. Lukin thought for a fleeting moment that he should start demanding his rank from these fools, but he was too tired and his mind a little too unbalanced for that right now.

"Gospodin Ketchum," Lukin said, shaking hands all around. "Where is young George?"

"He hunts," was Ketchum's response. Less than perfect, but it got the job done.

Lukin looked over at Rudinov. "What are the chances that the spot where my daughter is peeling bark just happens to be in the same area where Adams is hunting?"

"The odds are good," said Rudinov. "Upriver a couple days."

"My daughter is beyond my command, it seems."

Rudinov laid a hand on his shoulder. "Strength and courage, Captain."

There was a momentary worry that Anastasia might get a visit from Zia, but that seemed unlikely—she would be turning her attention to Denisov, which meant that he had to be warned, if he'd listen to reason.

When pleasantries were passed, the sleds unloaded and put away, and the dogs tied up for the summer, he crossed the courtyard with his gear slung over his shoulder and opened the door to the rooms he shared with Anastasia. Inside, the walls carried the faint scent of his daughter's residence and there were also the memories of little Ilya and how he and his son use to throw a blanket over themselves and call it the blanket house. The last time they had done this had been over in that very corner where Anastasia now had her bed behind privacy panels of birchbark stitched onto a willow frame.

"Jesus," he said to the empty room. A mosquito flew past him through the door.

"Lukin." It was Kennicott.

Lukin dumped his things on the floor and stood his musket against the kitchen counter. "Yes?"

The Yankee leader was framed in the bright light by the rectangle of the doorway. "I want ask you of trip over Fort Youcon."

"You've learned some Russian, I see."'

"Some, but I no speak good." His syntax was almost comically childish but Lukin was inclined to cut him some slack. Not everyone got patted on the head by a giant and bestowed the power of language, and for those who didn't it wasn't so easy to learn another language. One of God's many curses on the lives of men. And trying to do it as a grown adult could be a steep hill indeed. He was also, not incidentally, glad to have something to think about besides Zia and Anfisa.

He decided on a whim to try some English, something he'd fitted together in his head. "Kurila tell me you go up to British." It sounded so awful he couldn't help but chuckle at himself.

Kennicott's face brightened. "I want to take a small party of men upriver, maybe two or three plus myself, and make contact with the British at Fort Youcon. I spent a winter there back in fifty-nine, and I'll admit I'm keen to see the place again. You'll be coming with us, so perhaps you should see about securing a boat."

Lukin felt a sudden pointed need to go off somewhere by himself and stare at the river ice and ponder what he would say to Anfisa the next time he saw her. He was also not a little irritated by the high tone Kennicott put on when addressing him. Eager to extricate himself from the voluminous conversation, he blinked a couple times, then said, "I will see what is available. Would you excuse me for a moment?"

Kennicott cocked his head at Lukin. "Yes, of course. But come find me later, if you would."

"Will do."

Lukin walked out through the front gate and was halfway down to the river when he froze, quite literally in mid-stride. The Major had spoken to him in English, and he'd understood it perfectly. Not only that, but he'd been able to respond in kind. Many years ago the giant whose name sounded like aspen leaves in the wind had told him that he would be able to speak all the languages of the country. The tongue of the Quarrelers upriver and the Kolosh language of Sitka had been chasms he could never bridge, but now here was English, in his head and on his lips like he'd always known it.

He spun back to face the fort. The Company's flag with its three stripes of white, blue, and red and the Romanov royal crest flew above the bastions as ever. The ground seemed to have slid twenty feet to one side while he'd been looking elsewhere; the rumor of the sale now had to be true.

6

BEGUILED — A NEW UNDERSTANDING — RUNNING AWAY — PROVENDER FROM THE AWAKENING FOREST — MAMMALIAN DESIRE — REMEMBERING — NEVER GOOD ENOUGH — TWO LOVELY DAYS — SPRING FRESHET — VISITORS — A CHILLING REALIZATION — BACK AT NULATO — PRECAUTIONS — THE MOON IN VAIN — THE BIDARSHIK'S SUSPICIONS — WHERE IS KENNICOTT — 279 DEGREES — A CHRISTIAN OFFER

Two days after his arrival back at Nulato Lukin was sitting in his quarters eating the leftovers of a broiled goose and brooding over his encounter with Zia when Anfisa appeared at the open top of his Dutch door.

"Come in," he said, wiping his mouth on a more-or-less-clean kitchen rag he'd been using as a napkin.

Springtime sunlight filled the room and it was unthinkable to shut it out. She closed the bottom half of the door behind her and crossed the room. He stood and slipped his arms around her waist as she pressed up against him. She smelled of woodsmoke and birch rind and new green grass.

"Back so soon?" he said. "Not that I'm disappointed, mind you."

She smiled up at him. "How could I stay away?" Her eyes seemed slightly too large for her face as she batted her lashes at him.

"Oh stop," he said with a smile spreading over his own face, which in turn brought forth a giggle. Anfisa clapped a hand over her mouth in the most beguiling of gestures. It was something Lukin had grown to love seeing. *How could Yosif ever lose interest in this?* he thought.

"You trimmed your beard," she said.

"So I did." Lukin ran a hand over his close-clipped whiskers. There was more gray in them than he wanted to admit.

"How is fort life?"

"Insufferable. Kennicott won't stop pestering me about wanting to go upriver to Fort Youcon right after the ice breaks." Now that he could understand their English he was confronted daily with their racial arrogance. Ketchum, in particular, would not stop addressing him as *Boy,* though Lukin was at least ten years his senior. Ignorance had been bliss, and he was rapidly tiring of being treated as something less than human because his skin wasn't lily-white, all while they relied on him for even the most basic of things like small children in need of constant supervision. The worst part was that because they weren't Company employees he didn't have the authority to have them flogged for their insolence.

He wanted to tell all of this to Anfisa but was still unsure what to make of it all himself. And in the back of his mind was an idea that it was best to keep his newfound comprehension of English to himself. For the time being, at least.

"Want to go be free agents for a while?" she asked.

"What do you have in mind?" This seemed too good to be true. No doubt Denisov would come through the door at any moment and the whole thing would be thrown asunder.

"I know a spot up the Nulato River. We could build a canoe, shoot some ducks. Maybe get some muskrats too."

It sounded like the best idea Lukin had heard in about twenty years. "Where is this going?" he asked. "You and me?"

Anfisa closed her eyes, took a breath, then opened them once more. "I don't know. But I cannot bear to stand still with you."

* * *

They left later that day, before her husband could return and start issuing orders. Each carried a heavy pack, and by silent agreement they walked hard up the side of the river in the sunshine with the scent of newly exposed earth everywhere. They wanted more than anything to put distance between themselves and the fort, to say nothing of the world at large. Having grown up at Nulato, Anfisa knew the lay of the land better than Lukin, right down to the individual trees. He was happy to let her lead the way. Among other things it afforded him the opportunity to admire her curvaceous backside, which provided a welcome distraction from the sweaty shirt and vest under his pack.

Anfisa moved expertly through the trees, winding easily around willow thickets, clumps of rosehips, springtime puddles and mudholes. At the fork of the river she turned right and they continued for another mile to a maze of sloughs and linear ponds made by the river shifting its course and abandoning its former oxbows. A substantial hill rose behind them, forested with birch, spruce, and aspen.

"This is where we'll camp," she said, dumping her pack in a stand of aspen and cottonwood next to a wide sandbar. The water was running mostly over top of the dirty ice that had sagged down to the gravel bottom. This tributary was small enough that Lukin reckoned he could leap over it with a running start, not that he had any inclination to do so.

"Lovely spot," he said. "You've been here before, I take it." There were old signs of folks having camped here—axe-cut stumps, a birch tree with an old peeling scar long since healed over.

Anfisa stepped about six feet to her left and scraped aside the dead leaves from the previous fall with the toe of her moccasin. It revealed a fire ring sunk into the soil. “I used to come here with my family.”

“Looks like nobody’s been around for quite some time.”

“That’s because Larion killed everyone.”

“Ah.”

“I hid up here after the fight,” Anfisa said. “Until my Nowikaket kin came and found me.”

Lukin was silent for a moment, considering that his own misfortunes in life had been rather minimal compared to hers.

“I’m going to go find some birchbark for our roof,” she said, brushing strands of hair back from her forehead and re-tying her kerchief. “Maybe you could go see if there’s any food around.”

“Count on me.” He took up his musket from where he’d stood it against a tree.

She stood up on her toes and kissed him. “Come find me later.” She pointed at the hill behind them where the notch of a creek valley cut down to the river bottom. “I’ll be over there, along that little creek that runs down.”

Springtime as the ice was going out had always been Lukin’s favorite time of year. The snow was mostly gone and the mosquitoes were not yet out in force. And if your eye had to get accustomed to looking at the world once again without snow, it was lovely to behold the fresh grass poking up from the brown of last year’s thatch, the very brightest color of hope.

He made his way to one of the sloughs and killed two ducks in the small patch of open water at one end, lining up his shot to get them both. The others bolted, running off the surface of the water and then onto the edge of the rotting ice and taking wing as he retrieved their unfortunate companions with a long spruce pole. He detoured through a stand of aspen trees and dallied a bit looking for morels. He found nearly two dozen sprouting up from the leaf litter near a recent burn and tied them up inside a spare kerchief. He recalled Sava Golinov once making the point that it was wise to show up at a lady's fire with a gift, and Lukin had always found this to be true. The collective Denakeh word for mushrooms was *earth ears* and Lukin had never met a Dinneh person who would eat them for anything other than the occasional religious experience. The Russian side of his heritage, however, was inclined to find them delicious.

The sound of running water filtered through the trees from all quarters as he hurried along the hillside Anfisa had spoken of. *Ducks, green grass, a beautiful lady, and morels,* he thought. *What could be finer?* Desire propelled him onward.

At the base of the hill he moved slowly until he caught sight of Anfisa through the luminous white birch trunks. She was peeling a sheet of bark nearly as broad as the spread of her arms and having some difficulty with it. Before long she heard his feet and paused with the bark hanging vertically off the tree as he approached.

"That's a big piece," he observed.

Her scarf had been pulled back from her head. She reached behind her and pulled her long braid of hair out from underneath it. When she blinked at him it was patently obvious that she knew she was a hopeless flirt. "I could use the help of a strong man."

"Your wish is my command."

She let out a girlish sigh. "Such gallantry."

The bark had only been unwrapped about a third of the way around the trunk; the nature of Anfisa's difficulty was that this particular sheet wanted to split along the peeled edge. Lukin found a stick and used it to support the leading edge as he flexed the bark back on itself, which allowed her to get the bit of her axe in between the moist green inner bark and the dark outer rind. Gradually, the sheet pulled around the trunk until the final end came free. Lukin laid the sheet on the ground with the white side up for visibility. This was something his mother and aunts had taught him many years ago: It was all too easy to peel dozens of bark sheets, lay them on the ground with the moist brown inner side facing up as you moved to the next tree, and then not be able to find them all again because the color blended into the ground cover.

Anfisa touched the bright underbark, wet with spring sap like a sponge, then patted the trunk. She spoke a few words of thanks to the tree's spirit. The forest nearby was dotted with white rectangles of peeled bark.

She turned and looked at him. He'd been about to show her the morels but she blinked up at him and the buzzing in his trousers became impossible to ignore. She untied the kerchief from her neck and let it fall away. The neckline of her blouse was down off her shoulders under the straps of her fawnskin sarafan, and this was surely no accident.

They came to each other in a frenzy of hands, working at each other's clothing. Garments suddenly became impediments to the most ancient of urges. Her nipples tightened and pushed out when his lips found them. She gasped and ran her fingers through his hair. It was frenzied and unquestionably mammalian.

Afterward, they lay on the forest floor among the greening rosehips and listened to the birds. The dry leaves were warm from the sun but he could feel the cold damp ground just beneath them.

"God's own symphony," Anfisa said eventually.

"Pardon?"

"The singing of the birds. That's what my father always called it."

"Have you ever heard a symphony?" Lukin himself never had. It was music, he knew, played by a large group of musicians, but there was no such thing in Russian America.

"No. Only the birds."

"I've brought you something," Lukin said, reaching for his bundle of earth ears.

"I love presents." Anfisa lay on her stomach with her knees bent so that her feet kicked up loosely in the air behind her. She'd not bothered to take off the high-topped moccasins that came up over her knees; the soles were dark from the moisture of the springtime woods and inside this there seemed to be a mystery Lukin couldn't quite get his head around.

He passed her the mushrooms. She unfastened the knots in his kerchief that bound up the four corners.

"Morels!" she exclaimed. "Where did you find these?"

He composed his face into a mask of disaffected mystery. "A spot I know."

Back at their campsite Anfisa made tea and roasted the ducks by singing off all the feathers in the fire, then slathering them in mud and baking them directly on the coals. She poured seal oil into her sheetiron skillet and fried the morels until they began to crisp, then stirred in a little flour and water to make a gravy. They ate cross-legged by the fire from plates fashioned of birchbark and finished off the meal with the last of the kulitch she'd baked during Lent. The sugar supply was nearly finished after the long winter, which made such a treat all the more special.

Lukin sat with his back against a large cottonwood tree, watching the flames. Anfisa added more wood, then settled between his legs, reclining against his chest. The evening was just cool enough to require clothing.

"Ivan," she said.

"Yes?"

"Do you ever miss the Kuskokwim?"

It took him a moment to think this over. "I used to miss it a lot. Every single day. My first son is buried there."

"You looked so lost and forlorn when I first saw you at Nowikaket. I recall thinking you must have been terribly lonely without your country."

"I was."

"I was hiding in one of the caches, watching you come up the bank. You looked like a man with a weight of shame and anger on your shoulders. It seemed like you composed your face into a mask to avoid breaking into tears."

"I suppose I must have. It was a difficult time. Iriana was among those who blamed me for what happened at Fort Kolmakov." Lukin hadn't thought for some time about the Kolmakov mutiny that had upended his life; his mind had been occupied with other things. It was, he considered, not unlike the death of a loved one. You never truly forgot it, but with time the pain faded to the point where you could function.

"I've lived around Nulato and Nowikaket all my life," Anfisa said. "I can't imagine having to move away from the river. Back when Sava retired and moved back to the Gulf of Kenay, Yosif got really homesick. He started talking about moving back to Kenay or Kalifornsky Town when his retirement finally came up, and all I could think about was how much I didn't want to go."

"They say it's the best place in Russian America," said Lukin. "The best balance of climate and food and good soil."

Anfisa chuckled. "Well, Sava and Yosif say that."

Lukin drew in the scent of her hair. "So is Yosif still pushing for a move to Kenay?"

"No. Not since he married Sabrina."

"I see." He'd expected her to stiffen against him at the mention of this new, younger wife, but she didn't.

They watched the fire for a while. Deep in the forest a ruffed grouse cock drummed his wings to draw the attention of a hen. "Every single creature searches for love," Anfisa said when the drumming faded away.

Lukin smiled into her hair. "I think it was my memories that I missed as much as anything from Fort Kolmakov. There were a lot of unhappy things in my head when the Company demoted me and reassigned me to St. Michael. And then there was the fact that I was Semyon Lukin's son."

"I know what that's like." She shifted the tone of her voice to one of stern authority, wagging a finger at the far side of the fire. "Young lady, you are the daughter of the Bidarshik of Fort Nulato. I expect better from you than this!"

She smiled as Lukin chuckled against her. "You mean to tell me that Vasili Deryabin's daughter was never allowed to settle for close enough?"

He could see the back of her head move as she rolled her eyes. "Neither could Semyon Lukin's son, I'd wager."

"And the eldest son at that. Even now I hear people talk about what a great man my father was. I'm just the son who never could measure up."

Anfisa picked up a twig and snapped it in two, then snapped each piece again. He'd noticed this fidgeting habit of hers before; the Dinneh tribes generally regarded it as unseemly in a well-brought-up lady, but Anfisa was a grown woman and could fidget all she wanted to as far as he was concerned.

"Are you happy here?" she asked.

"I'm happy right now."

"Yosif told me you were hoping the Company would send you to build a trading station at Nuklukayet."

"That's what they keep telling me. But for now I have to settle for babysitting the Telegraph Men. They want me to take them up to Fort Youcon."

"Do you think it will happen?"

Lukin considered this, mulling over the fact that the project kept getting pushed back to the next summer and then the next. Also there was his newfound command of English, which was unsettling in a way he'd never quite experienced before. "Maybe someday. I've wanted to go have a look up the Tananah River for a long time. It would be nice to get to do it before I'm too old."

"It could happen, Ivan."

"Perhaps. Have you heard this rumor that the Yankee president wants to buy Russian America from the Emperor?"

Anfisa settled deeper into him. "Hush. I'm done speaking of ordinary things."

* * *

They spent two lovely spring days in the valley, shooting ducks and geese around the ponds and setting traps for muskrat. The evening of the second day Lukin stumbled across the prints of a black bear newly emerged from its den. He tracked it and brought it down with a head shot. Bear meat was taboo for Denakeh women, but Anfisa seemed to have no worries about eating it. "That's the best thing about being half and half," she told Lukin as she picked up another slice of roasted backstrap. "You get to choose the best parts of each side and forget about the rest."

The river continued running over top of the ice, making its peculiar sluicing sound. Lukin was blessed with deep sleep during these nights. He'd long since learned not to question things when he got to sleep a full night but just take it as a gift from God. What a pleasure to wake well-rested in the morning sunshine next to a beautiful naked lady with the birds singing and the river running and plenty of food.

It was two nights after he killed the bear that the dream came. There was a large fine house he recognized as the governor's log mansion in New Archangel. Crystal glasses, tablecloths trimmed with French lace. Rugs from Persia laid over the spruce puncheon floor. Glass windows with a downhill view of the bay and the town and the ships riding at anchor. There is a room with two more glass windows. A bed and a desk and there at the desk sits a youth of perhaps ten years in a clean white shirt and dark vest of Spanish cut. His hair is barbered close and there are a series of books open in front of him as he scribbles with a quill on a sheet of paper. A slate is propped in the window with mathematical equations chalked across it and there is a distinct sense that this pupil has just graduated to doing his exercises on paper. Footsteps sound in the hallway. Lukin watches as the young scholar turns in his chair and only then does he see his face. He is watching his father learn the mathematics of sea navigation. Ivan Lukin recalls the of-told story of how a Boston ship captain named Burnett found young Semyon living as a slave among the Yakutat Kolosh and purchased him and took him to New Archangel. A man in a well-tailored British-cut coat with a tall collar enters the room and bends over the youth's exercises. Lukin knows this man instantly—it is the Butcher, Aleksander Baranov. His balding head, his wide cheeks, his hawkish nose. His gray eyes show the icy calculus of an emperor, but for whatever reason he is fond of young Semyon. The boy lives in his house and he himself tutors him so he will have an education and be useful to the Company. This is good work, he says to Semyon. Keep at it. You are a smart one and this will take you to great things in life. There is a tap at the door. A Cossack workman holds an Aleut girl not much older than Semyon painfully by the arm. His long mustaches droop down below his chin as he speaks. She is ready for you, sir. Her hair is down and she wears a skirt, blouse, and stays of Mexican make, like so many of the women's clothes in the colony. Baranov favors her with a wolfish look, then straightens himself. Semyon keeps watching out the door and the girl's eyes meet his for a moment before she is dragged up the stairs to his mentor's bedchamber.

"Ivan, wake up."

He felt himself swimming upward, as if from the bottom of a deep pool. Something with tentacles curling below him seemed to be grabbing at his feet. The water was dark, stained with tannin and studded with gleaming bubbles of air and as he looked up in the struggle it seemed to get deeper and deeper over his head.

"Ivan."

He snapped his eyes open. There was Anfisa, the roof of their bark shelter above her. She was shaking him.

"What?"

"The camp is flooding," she said. "There must be an ice jam downriver."

Lukin sat up. Indeed, the fire pit just a few feet away was under two inches of water and the edge had started to soak Anfisa's bedding. Beyond he could see the river spilling its icy banks and the freshet filling in between the big cottonwoods.

"Shit," he said.

"Come on," she said. "We need to get everything to higher ground."

"Right."

They jumped into action, yanking everything away from the water as it rose around their ankles. Lukin wrapped whatever he could reach into their pile of blankets and caribou skins and raced up the hill behind camp. When he got back Anfisa was sloshing in water up to her calves as she hurried to disassemble the lean-to so the bark roof could be used for a new shelter. He helped her cut the spruce-root lashings and they grabbed the last few things, his musket among them, and got back up the hill.

"Hell's bells," she said as they stood panting next to the pile of their gear, watching through the aspen trunks as the water spread over the valley floor.

"No joke." Lukin drew a sleeve across his sweaty forehead. "That's a rude awakening."

"The birds have stopped singing."

Lukin's mind was still half in the dream and as he watched the water creep to the base of the hill he suddenly knew who had been holding onto his feet as he swam upward to the world. This flood was no accident.

"Zia," he said, taking up his musket. The gunpowder charge thankfully had not gotten wet. He slipped a cap over the nipple, then pushed three musketballs into the spaces between the fingers of his left hand for fast reloading.

"Ivan, what is it?"

He put his musket at halfcock, scanning the water and the trees it enveloped, searching for her dark form. Briefly, he reached into his jacket pocket where the lock of her matted hair from the fight rested next to the blue bead he'd carried for luck all these years. "There are things you need to know, my love."

She was wringing water from her blankets. "What must I know?"

"There is a creature following us."

"What creature?"

"Her name is Zia. She's been following me for years."

"Ivan, what are you talking about?"

Lukin smoothed his mustache with the back of his hand. Over all these years he'd never spoken of Zia and it was hard to know where to begin. "When I was in school at New Archangel with Yosif and Sava I used to skip classes and go to this little cove through the woods. Just to have some time to myself, you know?"

Anfisa nodded, waiting for him to continue.

"I was sitting on the beach one afternoon and she changed herself from a drift log into a girl."

"A girl?"

"I was thirteen and she was naked and beautiful."

She cocked an eyebrow at him. "Oh really."

"She tried to kill me, Fisa. To devour my soul and take me down into the water with her forever. The only thing that stopped her was that Yosif happened by and caught us." He'd been scanning the forest again as he spoke but looked back to find Anfisa watching him. "Ever since that day, there's been a face carved into the moon that watches me wherever I go. And she follows me. Wherever I happen to be she finds me near the water and wants to talk." Lukin was surprised by the emotion that filled his voice. "And she shows me things."

"What things?" Anfisa's voice might have had a jealous cast to it, but he couldn't be sure.

"Things about my family's history. About the colony. About my parents and my grandparents. About Baranov and the things he did."

"History lessons?"

"More like visions. Visions that I cannot seem to escape." It was not lost on Lukin that twice now Zia had seized his dreams when he'd been asleep next to Anfisa. His guess was that Zia had been thinking that his splitting up with Iriana was the opening she'd been waiting for, and now here was this new mortal woman in her way. Panic rose inside him as he realized the danger Anfisa was in.

"My father used to say that none of us can escape history," she said.

"I reckon that's why she's been showing me these things. She doesn't want me to escape. She wants to keep me shackled to her. Or maybe she's just been trying to wear me down all these years. Hell, I don't know."

"This creature has kept following you all the way up here? On the Kwifpak?"

"Yes. I saw her a lot on the Kuskokwim as well. She lives in the water, so she can go pretty much anywhere."

"Why the moon?" Anfisa scanned the sky above but the moon was nowhere in sight.

"What do you mean?"

"You said she uses the moon to watch you."

"I don't know why the moon. It controls the ocean tides, which might be an important thing to her. But I don't know. I really don't have many answers to give."

"She tries to seduce you?"

"In a manner of speaking, yes."

It was hard not to be affected by how stone-silent the forest had become as the water continued to fill the valley floor below and creep up the toe of the hill below them. There was no telling how high it would get before the ice dam downstream broke. "Why have you not sought out magic to drive her away?"

Lukin took a moment to formulate his answer with care. "Did you know that my father used to buy slaves whenever he encountered them and then set them free?"

"I've heard that."

"It's why he didn't have any money to retire on when he got old. The Kolosh kept him as a slave for a few years when he was a boy and it drove him to free as many people from bondage as he could."

"Iriana was a slave when you met, I'm told," said Anfisa.

"She was. And I suppose I've tolerated Zia all this time because I wanted to help her. To find some way to free her. She's a prisoner of some malevolent force."

"Or she is the malevolent force, maybe."

* * *

They saw no sign of Zia through the night but in the morning hours a canoe came paddling up the valley that had now turned itself into a lake. It was Anfisa who spotted it first. She shook Lukin awake from his dozing and pointed.

"Who is it?"

"It's my husband."

Lukin studied Denisov's form as he guided the craft between the trees. Eventually he came into the shallows and had to get out and wade up to the edge of the water, pulling the vessel behind him. He paused a moment and at his side a girl's figure rose from the silky liquid.

"There," Lukin said. They could hear the water sluicing off her skin as she walked up next to Denisov and pointed up the hill.

"So that's her?" Anfisa whispered. Down in the water through the trees Zia drew Denisov down and planted a lingering kiss on his mouth as he wrapped an arm around her. Looking up at him, she trailed a finger over his vest buttons.

"It is."

"She really needs to comb out her hair."

Lukin snorted the smallest of laughs. Anfisa scanned the hillside and her gaze stopped upon their location.

"She knows where we are," Anfisa whispered.

Lukin checked the sky for the moon but it had fled for the day. "Indeed. You have the axe?"

She looked around at their gear. "Shit."

"What?"

"I left it buried in that stump at camp. We were in a hurry."

"Well let's hope you don't need it. See her standing behind that spruce tree?"

"I think so."

Down the hill, Denisov called out to both of them.

"Should we answer?" Anfisa asked.

"Follow me." They rose and carefully picked their way down the slope. The morning sunlight was just spilling onto the water from over the ridgeline but they were behind the shadow line.

"Good morning, you two," Denisov said as they approached. Even above the waterline the ground was soft from the flood and their moccasins sank into it an inch or so at each step.

"Good morning, Bidarshik." Lukin had been trying to keep his eye on Zia as they descended but had lost sight of her among the tree trunks.

"Why the gun?"

"You're in the company of someone I know too well."

Denisov smirked. "So are you."

"I can't see her," Anfisa said quietly to Lukin.

"Me neither."

"See who?" Denisov said.

"What has the creature promised you?" Anfisa said.

"I don't know what you're talking about," his eyes turned colder than Lukin had ever seen them, "my rabbit."

"Why have you come here?" Lukin asked. He thought he saw a shape move behind a cottonwood trunk to their right. The direction hardest for him to turn and shoot. Beyond, Denisov's large canoe floated placidly in the flooded forest like a horse left in a pasture to graze.

"I am retrieving my wife and one of my employees who ran off together."

Lukin and Anfisa watched him. "I'm not going back to live with you and your second wife, Yosif."

His face became passive. "I don't expect you to. You have failed to give me any children, despite trying to fuck every able-bodied man on the Kwifpak. So you may go where you will."

Anfisa didn't seem to know how to react to this. "How quickly rumor does become fact," she said quietly.

"Are you going to challenge me to a duel?" Lukin asked.

"Don't be silly. We all have our dalliances. My wife is Creole, and you know the old saying. To share her with every man in town."

"I suppose I do."

"Get your things. You are coming back to the fort. Kennicott has been pestering me nonstop about your trip upriver. And your daughter has been carrying on with that Adams boy. A father should keep better control over his children."

"Don't presume to lecture me on fatherhood, Yosif Denisov."

"I am the bidarshik and I will lecture you on any topic I see fit."

Lukin had never so badly wanted to hit his old friend. The only thing that stopped him was the realization that it was very likely Zia who was saying these things through the apparatus of his mouth. Then it dawned on him: *She's promised him the one thing he wants above all else. She promised him children of his own. Children from her womb.*

Behind the cottonwood he spotted Zia watching them with one eye. Lukin spun on his left foot and raised his gun in a single motion and fired. Bark shrapnel flew into the air and he was already charging at her, pouring gunpowder into the barrel of his weapon and sliding one of the bullets from his left hand into the bore and slamming the butt against the ground to drive it down to the breech. He capped the gun and snapped it up to fire again but

Denisov tackled him and pinned him to the ground. Anfisa leapt onto Denisov and tried to wrench him away but she didn't have the strength.

It was Zia who pulled her away, dragging her by the ankles. Anfisa shrieked and punched like a feral cat. She got a leg loose and made a kick for her crotch and clawed at her eyes but Zia was far stronger and pinned her against a tree with a hand clamped over her throat and squeezing. Lukin bellowed with rage and tried to sink his teeth into Denisov's arm to get him off him but he couldn't quite reach and he couldn't shift his weight off him or reach his dagger. Zia had her face right up next to Anfisa's with the most savage of smiles as she squeezed the breath from her. Anfisa's legs flailed in the mud and leaves as she grew frantic and then her eyes bugged out as she started to fade.

Zia was focused on her work but stopped short when she noticed the yellowjacket buzzing around her face. She shied away, dropping Anfisa who collapsed in a heap at the base of the tree and sucked in a wheezing breath followed by a coughing fit.

Zia danced away from the insect as it kept hovering right in her face. She swatted at it. The yellowjacket dove to the side but kept pace as she backed up toward the edge of the water. She waded in, ducking and shying to one side, then another as the angry buzz followed her until she dove into the water and disappeared. It was the only time Lukin had ever seen her afraid of something.

The yellowjacket hovered for a moment over the ripples she'd left, then flew off into the forest. Denisov was distracted enough that Lukin was finally able to wrench himself free. Staggering sideways, he shouted after her, "*Get away from us! Leave her alone!*" Anfisa wheezed in another breath, trying hard not to break into another cough. Lukin ran over to her, keeping Denisov at the edge of his sight. "Concentrate on breathing," he said to her. "But don't say his name." The yellowjacket must have been sent by Tathyaldin, the Tananah shaman who evidently still considered Anfisa to be under his protection. That at least was a good sign.

Denisov rose and watched them from under his brow. "You two get in the canoe."

* * *

Things at Nulato became exceedingly uncomfortable after the encounter with Denisov and Zia, and neither Anfisa nor Lukin had any real idea of what to do about the situation. All the same, it was clear that Anfisa was in mortal danger. She spent only one night back at the fort in Lukin's quarters before deciding the best course of action for the time being was to leave and head up to Nowikaket to stay with her family, somewhere away from the main river. It didn't take Lukin long to decide that Anastasia should go with her.

"But Papa," she said, "I just got back from a trip. And I don't know anyone at Nowik—" her tongue tripped over the name.

"Nowikaket. *Kaket* means river in the Denakeh tongue. Look, I wouldn't be sending you away if it wasn't important. Anfisa has powerful magic protecting her, and it will protect you as well. You will know it's working when you see yellowjackets buzzing around."

Anastasia stared out the open door. Her lips flattened. It was a gesture that reminded him an awful lot of her mother, his first wife Natalia. "You saw this creature?" she said. "With your own eyes?"

"I've seen her many times. But now that the ice has broken I have to go upriver with the Telegraph Men, which means I cannot be here to protect you."

"You think Captain Denisov is that much of a threat?"

Lukin glanced out the doorway then lowered his voice. "He could use you to try and get to me. That's my biggest worry." He softened his eyes as best he could. "I know this is a tough hand to draw, but I have no doubt you'll see young Adams again."

She flushed and looked down at the table. Lukin frowned, thinking that at some point when she was a young child he had picked her up and set her down without realizing it was the very last time he would ever do so. Children grow up, and then she was too big for that sort of thing, and now they were here. And he had to find Tathyaldin.

* * *

Among the more maddening aspects of Zia's presence in his life was that there was no predicting when she would come; the moon had never given him any sign of this. Still, he watched the daylight moon in the mornings and evenings as the leaves popped from the trees and the days quickly lengthened, racing toward the breakneck fullness of summer. The work of the telegraph expedition seemed the most trivial of banalities compared to everything else in his life, not the least of which was worrying about his daughter and Anfisa. The Yankees were obsessed with their mission of running the wire upriver to the border of Rupert's Land and then down to the United States—it was all they talked about among themselves, and now that he could understand them it was impossible to ignore their prattle. The mission seemed more and more to Lukin like a fool's errand but he kept his opinions to himself.

The morning the ice broke in the Kwifpak Denisov invited Lukin into his quarters for breakfast with Sabrina and her children; he was the bidarshik and Lukin really didn't have the option of refusing, and Denisov knew this. Sitting at his table, he kept expecting his friend to show the wear and tear of having Zia inside his soul—perhaps dark patches under his eyes, yellowed teeth—but he appeared as normal, more or less. His eyes were a little more intense and his demeanor even more haughty than before, though that might just have been the result of Lukin and Anfisa making him a cuckold. Or perhaps he was congratulating himself for having got the better of Lukin in a fight.

"These men are spies," Denisov said of the Yankees while they were eating. "And I need you to watch them closely."

Lukin had briefed Stepanov on the movements of the Telegraph Men while at St. Michael for Easter and was aware that he would have to write a lengthy report for the governor when all the nonsense with the wire was over. Lurking behind this was the vexing question of what it meant that he could now understand their English conversation. Perhaps the Czar really was thinking of selling his overseas colony. But there was nobody to whom he could voice this concern. Certainly not Denisov. It took every ounce of fortitude Lukin possessed to sit at the man's table and address him civilly. How could the incident with him and Zia be explained to the Company or the Church if official inquiries were made? Denisov was the bidarshik and they would undoubtedly take his word over Lukin's if it came to that. Keeping things quiet seemed to be the best option for the time being.

"I have my instructions from Stepanov."

"And now you have instructions from me," Denisov said.

"I am around these Yankees all the time. More than you or any other man here except maybe Kurila. I see nothing in their actions that would suggest they are here as spies."

Sabrina stood to refill their teacups when there came a rapping at the open doorframe. George Adams stood in the opening.

Denisov held Lukin's eyes for a long moment before speaking. "Come."

Adams stepped inside, flanked by Frank Ketchum. "Have you seen Major Kennicott anywhere?"

"Not since yesterday," Denisov said, still looking at Lukin.

"Have you seen him?" Adams asked Lukin. He spoke in Russian; Lukin had been keeping his newfound understanding of English a close secret. One among many.

"I have not." Lukin stood and set his napkin beside his plate. "Come, I'll help you look."

"I gave you no leave to go," Denisov said. His voice was louder than really necessary in the kitchen.

Lukin turned to face him. "By your leave, Bidarshik. I should go help them find Kennicott."

"That's better. You are dismissed."

Outside everyone was moving around the yard, apparently searching for the Major. "When was the last time you saw him?" Lukin asked Adams.

"Frank said he saw him go outside for a smoke sometime in the night," Adams said, hooking a thumb at Ketchum, who in turn was talking with Laberge and a man named Pease.

"Could he have wandered off somewhere?" Lukin asked. Denisov stood watching from his doorway.

"Rudinov was on watch," said Adams.

"Anatoli!" Lukin called out in general to the courtyard. "Bring me Anatoli Rudinov."

Rudinov was asleep in his small house, getting a few hours of rest after pulling the graveyard sentry shift. He came stumbling and yawning into the yard a few moments later with his fellow workers directing him toward Lukin.

"Did you see Kennicott go out the gate?" Lukin asked.

"The Major? Yes." He yawned again. "I opened the gate to let him out sometime after two in the morning."

Lukin exited the gate with Laberge and Pease. They seemed at a loss and could do nothing but call out Kennicott's name.

"Major!" Laberge shouted through his cupped hands. "Major Kennicott!"

"Bob!" Pease called upriver. Lukin had picked up that Pease and Kennicott were friends from childhood, not unlike himself and Denisov, actually. *Bob,* he was quickly able to discern, was a nickname for Robert, the Major's saint name.

While the Yankees shouted, Lukin moved around looking for tracks. The silty sand was still muddy from the spring melt and it didn't take long to find the freshest pair of bootprints—stacked leather heels were worn only by Yankees and Russian officers. He followed them down the high bank; the impressions were still dark where the heels had dug into the damp sand below the dry top layer that faced the sky.

Laberge and Pease trotted up behind him. "His tracks," Lukin said in Russian, pointing.

"He must have just gone for a stroll and laid down for a nap somewhere," Pease said in English. "He's done that sort of thing since we were kids." You could tell he was trying to convince himself as much as anyone.

"Maybe so," Laberge said.

"His health has never been good."

Lukin watched them as they talked. They clearly had no inkling that he understood every word.

Kennicott's footprints turned downriver. Lukin beckoned for Pease and Laberge to follow him. The prints led over the sand, weaving around the blocks of ice that had been left stranded on the bank. They were a couple hundred yards down from the fort when Pease cried out, "There!"

It was the Major's boots he'd spotted, poking out from behind an old rootwad that had been dragged along the beach by the grinding of the ice. Coming around the stump they found him lying on his back with his arms slightly spread.

"Bob?" said Pease, getting down on one knee next to his friend.

Robert Kennicott's eyes were closed to just the barest of slits. It was obvious at a glance he was not having a nap. His lips were parted in a way that left Lukin with the impression that his final word had been simply, "Oh!" His brass compass lay open next to him, and in a patch of loose sand he appeared to have used a forefinger to write a bearing: 279°. Whatever it meant had been lost to the wind.

Laberge shouted and waved an arm over his head to catch the attention of the others who were out searching. Pease's face went ashen and seemed to sink into itself. Just to be sure, Laberge knelt and held the back of his wrist above the Major's lips. No hairs stirred. Laberge unbuttoned Kennicott's vest and pressed an ear to his heart. A few moments later he drew back onto one knee. "Charlie, I'm sorry," he said to Pease. "He was as fine a man as I've ever known."

There were footfalls on the gravel behind them. It was Adams. "He's dead?" he said in Russian to Lukin.

Lukin nodded. "Look at those marks in the sand. He was sitting here taking a compass reading. Then he fell and died."

Adams blinked a few times, as if the whole scene was slightly more than he could accept. Lukin crossed himself. "Let us go tell the others."

Laberge rose and made what Lukin recognized as the Catholic sign of the cross, starting from the opposite breast as the Orthodox one he knew. "Someone should stay with him."

* * *

Lukin and Kurila spent the rest of the day splitting planks from a spruce log and planing them down to build a coffin for the Major. They caulked the seams with oakum and a mix of spruce pitch, grease, and charcoal, the same amalgam used to seal the seams of a bark canoe.

It took most of the day and when they finished he sent Kurila off for supper and went to knock on the door of the house the Telegraph Men occupied. Laberge let him in; they had the Major wrapped in a blanket and laid atop some planks set over a pair of sawhorses. Every face was gloomy. Death was all too common in the world but it was plain to see the Yankees had held their leader in high regard and keenly felt his passing.

He beckoned Adams over to him. The drawn faces of men who felt far away from home turned toward them.

"I have the coffin ready," he said.

Adams pursed his lips.

"How are you doing?"

Adams no longer looked like such a boy. He drew in a long breath. "Not well. But death comes to us all."

"True. I want to ask you something."

"Yes?"

"I notice you have all been praying. Would you like me to recite the funeral liturgy for the Major? I know he was not of the Orthodox faith, but I would be happy to do this."

Adams translated for the room. Frank Ketchum came over. "Thank you," he said in his halting Russian. "But Kennicott goes home. On boat. To Shee-kah-go."

"What is Shee-kah-go?"

"The town where his from," Adams said.

Lukin silently hoped they weren't going to ask him for help with embalming the man's body. Not that they had anywhere near enough salt to do this.

"We elected Frank Ketchum as our acting captain until the next group of men arrives in the fall," Adams said.

Wonderful, Lukin thought.

Ketchum reached inside his vest and withdrew a folded letter. Its red wax seal had been broken. "Major leave orders for if he die."

"He said for you to go up to Fort Youcon with Frank and Mike," Adams said. "The rest of us are going to take the Major down to St. Michael and be there to meet the supply ship."

Lukin folded his arms loosely over his chest, wishing he was anywhere but here and wondering if there had been any change in the distance of the watching moon. He could feel Denisov's eyes upon him from somewhere outside.

"When we go up river?" Ketchum asked.

"I'm ready when you are. But do not worry about that for now. What matters is devotion to God and your friend's soul. I shall pray for him." He turned to go. "The coffin is in the boathouse whenever you require it."

7

UP TO SEE THE BRITISH — TALK ALONG THE RIVER — THE HUDSON BAY FACTOR — A GIFT FOR LANGUAGES — BACK TO THE BERING SEA — SMOKE IN THE CHIMNEY — MORE TELEGRAPH MEN (WITH SUPPLIES) — THE STRUGGLING GARDEN — LOVE LIKE A BIRD FLIES AWAY — THE SCIENTIFIC CORPS — MORE BIGOTRY — RUSSIAN JUSTICE — CAMERA PHOTOGRAPHICA

The current of the Kwifpak was as indifferent as ever. Adams and most of his workmates had departed to take Kennicott's body down to Fort St. Michael, which left Ketchum and Lebarge as a minority at the fort. They were chomping at the bit to get on the water. Lukin had wanted to postpone the journey until the king salmon made it to the middle river for the fairly obvious reason that they could have fresh food along the way, but the two Yankees would not hear of it.

"These Russians are about the laziest bunch I ever did see," he heard Lebarge say to Ketchum after they made it clear to him in their childishly silly Russian that they would not stand for any more delay now that the river was open.

"He's got himself a fine little piece of ass," Ketchum commented with a catty look. "That first wife or whatever of Denisov's. I seen them going off together a couple times before she went upriver."

Lukin at the time was sighting down the shank of a bidarka paddle that had warped over the dry winter, assessing how much work it would take to steam-bend it back into place, or if he should just make a whole new paddle, or if maybe there was another one laying around he could swap it out for. Dogs, tethered for the summer, yowled in the background. For all the kindness he'd shown them when their boss died, this kind of behavior was his payment, but then he'd learned by now not to expect better. No good deed goes unpunished, but it took quite a bit of concentration on his part to keep his eyes fixed on his work instead of stalking over and swinging the thin edge of the paddle square into Ketchum's face.

Keep your eyes on your work, he told himself. By now, given his comprehension of their language, there was no doubt in his mind that the sale of Russian America was indeed going to happen and his country would be filled up with Yankees. Behind this he could only wonder if all their people were as crude, loudmouthed, and aggressive as these two. Even young Adams had a peculiar brashness to his demeanor at times that Lukin found off-putting. And then there were all the stories you heard of the brutal ways they dealt with Natives in their own country. In his darkest fears, the ones that came when he was awake in the wee hours, he wondered if bloodshed and slaughter was to become the new norm, something the colony had not seen since the days of Baranov's reign of terror. The thought chilled him to his very center.

Lukin felt them watching him. He looked up from his work, and for lack of anything better to say held out his fist with the thumb pointed skyward. *Up yours, you helpless fools.*

They departed the next day in a three-hatch bidarka, waving to the gathered crowd as they pulled themselves into the river with their three paddles; Lukin had straightened the crooked one, but made sure Lebarge got it. "A boatman's paddle is like his wife," he told him in Russian. "You must keep her close to you at all times, and not try to trade her away." This was pure bullshit, pulled straight from ass and presented as a hard and fast rule of life on the Kwifpak. Still, it had the intended effect. Lebarge took the paddle and didn't complain about its clumsy balance.

The long linear boat skimmed lightly, if not quite easily, upstream. Lukin coached his charges as best he could on technique and called out commands to keep their paddling in rhythm with his own. By the third day, blisters had raised on their palms, but they were making nearly twenty miles between breakfast and supper. At that rate, five days would get them a hundred river miles. Lukin's trip to Fort Youcon in 1862 had taken most of the summer but he'd been paddling alone in a bark canoe, and lining it against the current much of the way. Three paddles in a bidarka made for a much faster trip.

Anfisa and Anastasia were not at Nowikaket when they stopped there, but the local grandmothers assured him she was safe. They appeared to have been apprised of the situation with Denisov and Zia. Lukin had been looking forward to feeling Anfisa pressed up against him and running his hands down over her lovely backside, but then he was accustomed to disappointment in life.

The talk on everyone's lips was of the Yankees. The rumor about the sale of the colony had reached the ears of the Dinneh, and nobody seemed to know what to make of it, other than that there would be different white men for them to deal with. More than one person Lukin encountered was irked at the prospect of having to learn another damn white man language.

"Nobody knows anything for sure," he said to them. "Rumors fly like bats at dusk." It all felt like a lie because it was a lie.

* * *

Nobody had arrived at Nuklukayet when they passed the mouth of the Tananah River. They pulled into shore to make a fire and have a little tea.

"Get us wood, Ivan," Ketchum said to Lukin when they beached the boat.

"Get it yourself." Lukin was hunkered down to examine a seam on the bidarka's skin shell. Fresh water was hard on the hull of a skin boat and it required constant maintenance.

"You get wood!" Ketchum said, waving a hand at the driftwood scattered around the beach. "It's easy."

"No, you get wood," Lukin snapped. "I'm busy fixing the boat that carries your dumb ass."

"You are lazy!"

"Yeah," said Lukin, turning his attention back to the seam, "I sure am."

Ketchum stalked off in a huff and started breaking off branches with Lebarge. The repair was a minor one, though necessary, involving an awl and thread and a mixture of grease, charcoal, and spruce pitch. As he worked he kept stealing long looks up the Tananah and wondering where Tathyaldin was and how he could find him. There was also a south-facing aspen hillside on the far bank of the Tananah that kept drawing his eye. It would be a fine site for a trading station.

He joined his companions at the fire when he'd finished. Lebarge had the tea made and ready to pour. "What you look at?" Lebarge asked him.

Ketchum was rather pointedly not looking at him. Lukin looked over at Lebarge, then back up the Tananah.

"Just wondering what's up there," he said, pointing with his pipestem.

"You ever go up that river?"

"No, not more than a few hundred yards."

Lebarge leaned in. "Where it goes? Can wire go there to make fast trip to British lands?"

Lukin frowned, thinking that this would all be so much easier if he could just speak English.

"Perhaps. But nobody knows where the headwaters are. It might run off course a thousand miles from where you need to go."

* * *

Fort Youcon surprised Lukin because it seemed to be not as far up the Choonjik River as he remembered. There were a few unsettling moments when he wondered if his memory was beginning to fail him, but then he noticed the buildings looked brand new. In fact, some of them were still under construction. When he squinted upriver, he could just barely make out the original palisade; the river seemed to have shifted and eroded the bank so that the current was cutting under the foundations. The logs nearest the river had already toppled, and the end of the store was leaning well off-kilter. It was obvious enough that the fort had been moved. Absolutely nothing, it seemed, was permanent in this life.

The British trader he remembered as being named Jones had been replaced by a Scotsman named MacDougall. He came down to the bank with most of the fort occupants to meet the telegraph party. From the lack of large canoes on the shore, Lukin surmised that their summer freight had not yet come down the Choonjik.

"You are Russians?" he said in English.

"We're Americans," said Ketchum.

The Scotsman frowned. "Americans?" Lukin could hear that he spoke his English with a markedly different pronunciation from that of the Yankees. He steadied the boat while Lebarge and Ketchum climbed out. The Canadian boatmen eyeballed the lines of their vessel, a construction alien to them.

"We've come with the Western Union Telegraph Expedition," Ketchum explained.

"Ah yes," said MacDougall. "We've been expecting you." He looked at Lukin again. "But I thought there would be more of you."

"We have more men coming this summer. I'm Frank Ketchum and this is Mike Lebarge."

"James MacDougall, at your service. Who's this chap here?"

"That's our Russian. They gave him to us as a guide. His name's Lukin."

Lukin could hear it in the Yankees' voices that they were relieved to be able to speak their own tongue with someone in the country, which was not exactly a surprise. He rose from the rear hatch and planted his paddle in the sand and vaulted lightly onto the dry part of the beach.

"Lukin, eh?" MacDougall looked him over.

"Ivan Semyonovich Lukin." He put his hand out and MacDougall shook it.

"He doesn't speak any English," Lebarge said.

MacDougal was still looking at Lukin. "I believe this man is the Siwash who came up here to spy on my predecessor and then tried to defect."

"Is that a fact?" Ketchum said. Lukin's heartbeat froze in his veins for a second.

The Hudson Bay man smirked a little. "He's like all Russians. Backward and servile. It's quite easy to run circles around them, as you have no doubt found."

Lukin found himself far less embarrassed than simply pissed-off. The words came in English before he could check them. "Captain MacDougal, you and I both know this fort is built on Russian soil. Everything west of the 141st meridian belongs to the Czar."

All eyes stared at him, astonished. He'd tipped his hand and there was no point holding back now. "You have been trespassing and stealing revenue from my employer for nearly twenty years. So I will thank you to spare me your condescending rhetoric. You, sir, have no ground to stand on here."

"You speak English?" Laberge said.

"I have a gift for languages, Mister Laberge."

* * *

By September he was back at St. Michael, having returned down-river with Laberge and Ketchum all the way to the Kwifpak mouth and then up the coast to the fort, a voyage he'd never actually made before. There was a pleasure of fitting together the pieces of his geographical knowledge but it didn't quite leaven the sight of the new American ship riding at anchor in the canal. Smoke rose from the chimney of his old house but he noticed that Iriana was not among the crowd that gathered for them on the beach. Stepanov of course was there, moving about and sharing pleasantries with the Telegraph Men. There was a new Creole lass with him, easily young enough to be his daughter.

Lukin had just greeted Kurila and George Adams and the others when Pamilan came up to him and they embraced in a full-force hug. "How is Iriana?" Lukin asked him quietly when they could get away from everyone else.

"She's not well, I'm afraid."

"What's wrong?"

"She's coughing a lot. She can barely get out of bed."

Lukin looked again toward the old house he'd built so many years before right after Fort Kolmakov and the inquest and the move to St. Michael. "Is she staying warm?"

"My wife has been helping her out. She fires the pitchka every other day. Cooks for her a little."

There was excitement among the expedition crew because a new wave of workers had arrived for the big push to start hanging the wire. "These new Telegraph Men have even more gear than last year," Lukin said, gesturing at the piles of crates, boxes, and spools of wire—nearly two hundred spools—stacked up in the grass above the tideline.

"Don't I know it. Stepanov has had me and my boat crew bringing this stuff in for the past week. We just finished yesterday."

"I see I timed our arrival exactly right."

Pamilan smirked and raised his eyebrows. "You need a place to stay?"

"Yes, if you're offering."

"Our door's always open."

"Thanks. I'll be around in a little bit." He figured he might as well get it over with.

He stepped up into the grass and felt the chilly tundra wind bite through his jacket as he made his way up the path to the house. It felt a bit like going to visit a government minister. The walls needed paint and while the garden had been planted it was full of weeds and the potatoes seemed to be the only things that had survived.

It was odd to rap on what had once been his own front door. There was silence for the longest time and he was about to open the door and call inside when he heard coughing. Eventually the latch clattered in its track and the door was pulled inward.

"Good afternoon, Iriana."

She said nothing, just looked at him with the bleakest of expressions with a shawl pulled tight over her chest. A sour, sweaty odor rolled out from the open door.

"I'm around for a few days. I thought I'd look in on you."

"I was asleep."

He wasn't sure precisely what to do. She hadn't invited him in and showed no sign of doing so. Then again, that wasn't any big surprise.

Iriana bent into a coughing fit, covering her face with the crook of her elbow. She was almost over it when another one came and it seemed she might just topple over. Purely out of instinct, Lukin reached out to steady her but she pulled away.

"Did you think you would stay here?" she asked when she'd caught her breath.

Lukin shook his head. He managed a small smile. "I just wanted to see how you were doing."

"I was asleep," she repeated.

"Do you have enough to eat?"

"Yes."

Love like a bird flies away, Lukin thought for not the first time, frowning slightly at the sight of the kitchen countertop behind his wife. The place had never really been his home. He'd known fur traders who after so many long absences from their families preferred to just stay out in the woods as much as possible, sending their pay to their wives less a little money for grog, tobacco, and a new suit of clothes every now and then. He'd never really understood that phenomenon until this very moment. Love it seemed could only accomplish so much in the world, and he didn't know what to do with that notion.

"I'll send someone around to dig up your potatoes," he said.

"As you like."

* * *

The news of Kennicott's death came as a shock to all the new Telegraph Men, but there was no time for them to mourn. Their supply ship departed for San Francisco and they had to get themselves organized for the trip to Unalaklit before the sea froze over. Stepanov seemed to spend much of his time moving back and forth between his office and the waterfront, but he also seemed to be avoiding Lukin, aside from calling him into his office to brief him on the happenings of the expedition.

"These men certainly don't sound like spies," he said, rotating his teacup on its base upon the desktop. He sat in a reclining position with one leg crossed over the other and the knee propped against the edge of the wood.

"Yet everyone keeps insisting they are."

"Mm."

They sat in their chairs, not looking at one another. There came a knock at the door.

"Come in," Stepanov called.

The door opened and George Adams stepped in with a tall, gangly fellow at his heels. He was one of the new arrivals and looked to be barely a year or two older than Adams.

"Bidarshik," said Adams, "This is William Healy Dall. He is leads the expedition's scientific corps." Word had got around among the Telegraph Men that Lukin had learned to speak good English, but Stepanov had no comprehension of the language at all.

The bidarshik rose to shake the man's hand. "Mikhail Stepanov. Good day, Gospodin Dall."

Dall clasped his hand and Adams pointed at Lukin, still sitting in his chair. "And this is Ivan Lukin. He's been our guide and pilot this past year."

Lukin rose and put out his hand, but Dall did not take it. Instead he favored him with a smirk that Lukin recognized as the look of a man who thought himself superior to those with darker skin. He'd just about had his fill of such men.

"What can I do for you?" Stepanov said to Dall.

"Some of your men have been breaking into my supplies of ethanol for preserving specimens."

Lukin of course understood this, but he waited patiently while Adams translated for the bidarshik.

"Breaking into it? What do you mean?"

"They steal a jar of it to get drunk. I caught two of them last night."

"Ah, I see." Stepanov beckoned the Yankees out into the courtyard. Lukin followed out of hope he could get away.

"Can you point out the men to me?" Stepanov asked.

Dall looked around, then indicated a convict workman whose name Lukin didn't know. "He was one of them. In the gray cap."

"I will see to it he gets a beating. And that he reveals the identity of his accomplice.'"

Dall seemed slightly shocked by this, but Lukin didn't care enough to wonder about it any further. Across the courtyard there was an American setting up some apparatus atop a folding tripod. Lukin's first thought was that perhaps it was a transit, but then why would a transit be covered with a black cloth?

"What's he doing there?" Stepanov said, pointing.

"That's Mr. Ryder, our photographer," Dall said. Adams relayed this for Stepanov.

They watched as Ryder withdrew the cloth and fiddled with the instrument. Stepanov, suddenly excited as a small boy, stepped forward for a better look. "Is that a camera photographica?"

"It is," Dall replied.

Ryder trotted over to where some workmen and a few Malimiut women were moving around the courtyard. "Hold still, if you please," he directed, though of course they knew not a word of English. He tried to make himself understood through hand gestures, which proved ineffective.

"Hold still while he draws your images with light!" Stepanov shouted over to them.

Satisfied, Ryder held up an index finger, then ran back to his instrument, ducked under the cloth, and counted aloud to three.

"Alright, thank you!" he said when he stood up again. He moved his camera photographica over toward Lukin, Stepanov, Adams and Dall. "Gentlemen, may I make a photograph of you?"

Lukin thought his boss might actually clap his hands with glee. "Of course!" the bidarshik said.

Ryder set the tripod into the muddy ground, then arranged his subjects in the formation he wanted, standing four across, shoulder to shoulder. Lukin ended up on Stepanov's left, with Adams at his own left and Dall on the bidarshik's right. He wasn't sure what was expected of him and felt vaguely nervous and agitated. From the corner of his eye he could see Stepanov buttoning up his jacket and doing his best to look regal, like a man in command of an entire world. A lesser Baranov, perhaps. Lukin watched a couple seagulls flying past as Ryder repositioned the camera a few feet further back.

He fingered the blue bead and the lock of Zia's hair inside his jacket pocket. "What am I supposed to do?" he whispered to Adams in English.

Adams pointed at the camera. "You look into that lens there."

The front of the camera box held a wafer of glass, not unlike the lens of a telescope. Sunlight glinted off it ever so slightly.

"Alright, gentlemen," Ryder said from beneath the black shroud. "On three—One. Two. Three."

The finished photograph showed a Russian Creole of modest stature in caribou leather pants and one hand resting in the pocket of his wool jacket, his eyes wide and mouth slightly ajar as if utterly bewildered by life itself.

SEASONS OF WANT AND PLENTY:

Points of Culture and History

Baranov, that is, Aleksander Andreovich Baranov, (the Butcher, as Lukin and his companions often style him) was the first general manager of the Russian America Company. He had previously worked for Grigori Shelhikov, the Company's founder and president, on Kodiak Island where he established a methodology of systematically brutalizing Native people in the quest for sea otter pelts. After his appointment in 1799 he expanded the Company's interests eastward to the Alexander Archipelago (what is today known as Southeast Alaska) by fighting the local Tlingit people to a draw near the present-day city of Sitka (formerly New Archangel).

Latter-day historians have described Baranov as a "complex man," which is what mainstream writers usually say about vile white men who did terrible things in history. Baranov's methods were brutal, even by the standards of the day. He kidnapped wives and children to ensure obedience from husbands and fathers. He raped Native women and encouraged his men to do the same. He split up Native and Creole families by force as suited his whims and purposes, often sending husbands as far away as California and Hawaii against their will. Taking their families with them was never an option; the women and children had to stay under the governor's watchful eye. The fact that he provided contracts that specified payments to their widows and orphans does not change the essential fact that he treated these folks more or less as slaves.

Baranov was removed from power in 1818; after this, the colony was administered by Russian naval officers who served five-year terms on loan from their military service. Aleksandr Baranov died of illness at sea on his way back to face punishment in Russia.

Bidar and bidarka refer to the two most common kinds of boats used by the Russians in their North American colony. A bidar was a large open boat made of walrus skin (*laftak*, in the colonial argot) stretched drum-tight over a wooden frame. It could be moved either by sail or by pairs of oarsmen. This craft was a modified form of the oomiak of the Yup'ik and Inupiaq peoples.

The bidarka was essentially what twenty-first century readers would call a kayak. Like the bidar it was made from laftak stretched over a wooden frame. Bidarkas were originally adopted from the Unangan people of the Aleutian Islands in the 1700s, and proved so handy that the Russians built and used them everywhere they went in Alaska. They were made in configurations with one, two, and three hatches. Boats with laftak shells required regular maintenance to stay watertight, but when used in freshwater for extensive periods the skin would start to break down if not greased every day. Because of this, Russians on the interior rivers often made use of birchbark canoes built in the Athabascan Indian style, with flat bottoms and raked sides.

Bidarshik was the title given to fort managers in Russian America. In the earliest days of the colony, the term referred to the captain of a fleet of bidars (see above). A bidarshik had absolute authority over all of his subordinates, much the same as a ship's captain. There were, at least in theory, limits to what actions he could take and what punishments he could mete out. But God was up in Heaven and the Czar was far away.

Creoles in Russian America were people of mixed Russian and Native parentage. The Russian America Company encouraged its employees to marry and be fruitful with Native women, though how consensual these unions were is perhaps an open question. The Company was tacitly following a proven strategy of the Russian Empire from its conquest of Siberia: impregnate the local women (willingly or not) and produce a class of mixed-blood children who could speak the Native language, understand the culture, and serve as intermediaries, but would remain loyal to the Empire and to Russian cultural norms. The point is often made by historians that there were never more than 800 or so ethnic Russians in Alaska at any given time during the Russian period, but the population of Creoles was much more substantial. They constituted, in effect, the colonial citizenry, and were not infrequently placed in high positions of authority.

The word *Creole* was derived from the Spanish *criollo,* and may have been borrowed from the Spanish settlers of California with whom the Russian America Company had semi-regular interaction. It appears in printed Russian material as early as 1816. Those designated as Creoles paid no taxes. They and their children had the right to an education, paid for by the Company, though it could be argued that the Company provided this education mainly as a way of securing competent employees, something they struggled with throughout their existence.

People of mixed Russian and Native ancestry are still very much resident in Alaska. In recent years, the term Creole has come to be seen by some groups (though not all) as a racist legacy of colonialism in general, and the Russian occupation more specifically. I have elected to use it in these books for the simple reason that Ivan Lukin and his mixed-blood contemporaries in the 1860s most likely would have self-identified as Creole. Not only was it the term in everyday use in their world, it was the official legal designation of their social caste, no small item in pre-Soviet Russia.

Dinneh is a variation of the word *Déné,* which in turn refers to the Native Alaskan people more commonly known today as Athabascans. (In Canada, Déné is the preferred term.) Northern Athabascan people, speaking a plethora of related languages, occupy the boreal forest across a vast swath of the northern part of North America; the western half of this range encompasses Alaska's Interior. The word *Athabascan*, it should be noted, is not their word. It is an Anglo corruption of a Cree place name—Lake Athabasca, in northern Alberta—and was first coined in 1836 by the armchair ethnographer Albert Gallatin.

In the 1860s, Athabascan people were nomadic, moving frequently around their country to find food. Often they carried nothing but their weapons, an axe, a kettle, and their bedding. Wives and mothers would have their sewing kits. Whatever technology they needed beyond that was made on the spot as needed from wood, leather, stone, or whatever else was at hand; as Lukin's Athabascan mother points out to him, camping gear is much easier to carry inside your head than on your back.

Early accounts from explorers along the lower Yukon River (or the Kwifpak, as the Russians knew it) often make note the ethnic differences between Athabascan people and the Yup'ik people of the coast and delta region. More often than not, the ethnonym they record is some version of *Dinneh.* Modern-day Athabascan people in Alaska divide themselves into thirteen different groups, each speaking a different language. Among these are the Tanana, Deghitan (formerly known as the Ingalik), Upper Kuskokwim, and the Koyukon. In Lukin's world, the latter two are known by the terms Koltsan and Denakeh, respectively.

Fort Kolmakov, also known as Kolmakovski, was a Russian America Company trading station on the middle Kuskokwim River, near the mouth of the Hohlitna River and the modern village of Sleetmute. It was established in 1833 by Fedor Kolmakov and Ivan Lukin's father, Semyon Lukin (both Alaska-born Creoles) after a series of explorations and trading trips to the Kuskokwim that started in 1816. Initially the station was just a small cluster of cabins, but in 1841 the operation was moved across the river and built into a more substantial facility. The location was a strategic point at the boundary between the Athabascan and Yup'ik worlds.

Semyon Lukin would spend the rest of his career with the Company managing this settlement and the fur commerce that flowed through it. His oldest son, Ivan Lukin, was tapped to succeed him; he probably seemed like the logical choice, having worked there with his father almost since the post's founding. But

Ivan Lukin doesn't seem to have been, in modern parlance, management material. The Company relieved him from his duties for mismanagement and reassigned him to Saint Michael.

Fort Nulato was first established in 1839 by a Creole trader from Kenai named Malakov. His fort soon caught fire and burned to the ground. Vasili Deryabin rebuilt the post in 1842 and spent the next several years buying furs along the Kwifpak/Yukon River. At the same time, he searched constantly for the river's source. Deryabin was killed in 1851 when the Koyukuk River Athabascan chief known as Larion and several of his followers sacked and burned the fort. It was rebuilt soon after and continued to serve as the hub of Russian trade on the Kwifpak/Yukon River until the sale of the colony to the United States.

Ikogmiut Mission, known today in Alaska as Russian Mission, was the parish headquarters of the Russian Orthodox Church on the lower Kwifpak/Yukon. The name refers to the local Ikogmiut Yup'ik people. The Russian America Company also operated a trading station there, not the least because the settlement commanded the portage trail between the Yukon and Kuskokwim rivers. From Ikogmiut, a single Orthodox priest had to service a parish several hundred miles in circumference.

Kamelik was colonial Russian slang for a type of raincoat invented by the Unangan people of the Aleutian Islands. It was made from the small intestine of a sea lion that had been split and dried. This long strip of intestine would be sewn into a spiral shape that formed the body and sleeves of the garment, along with a hood. The finished product resembled a crinkly knee-length hoodie. Originally the hem of the garment was made to be secured around the rim of a bidarka, which would then form a watertight barrier to keep water from pouring into the boat's hatch when paddling at sea.

Kolosh is the name the Russians applied to the Tlingit people of Southeast Alaska after their initial hostile encounters. Not surprisingly, the modern Tlingit don't care for the name, and never did, which is putting things mildly. The Tlingit of Lukin's day lived in large communal houses framed with large timbers and covered over with split cedar planks. Their villages were almost always by the seaside in sheltered harbors; food from the ocean and the forest was abundant in their country (and still is), which in turn supported a large, sedentary population, even by 19th century standards.

Kwifpak River was the name the Russians adopted for the Yukon River. Because their early explorations moved upstream from the coast, they naturally enough adopted the name used by the Yup'ik (or Yupiak, in an older spelling) people who lived around the delta and the lower river. The search for the source of the river became an obsession for a handful of Russian traders, chiefly Vasili Deryabin of Nulato. The British Hudson Bay Company, approaching from the east by way of the Porcupine River (also known as the Choonjik River), also chose a name used by the local people they encountered: Youcon, spelled today as Yukon.

Malimiut is a cultural division of the Yup'ik people of western Alaska. The Yup'ik in turn are one of the broad divisions of the people who used to be called Eskimos, along with the Inupiaq, Sugpiaq, and Chupik.

The Malimiut live around Norton Bay and the Saint Michael area. Other Yup'ik groups mentioned in this series include the Kitagmiut and Kuskowagmiut of the Kuskokwim River, and the Ikogmiut of the lower Yukon. Any name that ends in the suffix *-miut* denotes Yup'ik or Inupiaq people.

Nuklukayet (pronounced Noo-clew-ka-yet) lies at the mouth of the Tanana River where it joins the Yukon. For generations prior to the arrival of Europeans, Nuklukayet was a meeting place for all the Athabascan people of the middle Yukon drainage. It is often described in historical literature as a trade fair, but it was much more than that. After a long winter of hustling a living in the forest, people wanted to camp out on the beach, catch lots of salmon, and reunite with friends and family they hadn't seen since last year. Maybe even get an occasional nap while the grandparents watched their kids. Time at Nuklukayet was the closest thing these folks had in their lives to a summer holiday, though there was always the imperative to catch and dry enough salmon to last the winter.

Pitchka furnaces have a long and storied tradition in Russian culture, and this was brought over to Alaska. They were constructed of stone and mortar, usually in the center of a dwelling, and were engineered to retain heat through thermal mass. Some pitchkas were as big as a car. In former times they were as universal as modern oil or gas furnaces, but they also did double duty as the hearth and primary cooking appliance.

Russian America was the official name in the Russian Empire of the colony that would become Alaska. The Danish explorer Vitus Bering, sailing for the Russian government, is credited with discovering Alaska in 1741 (in much the same way that Columbus "discovered" the Americas). In his wake, private companies of Siberian fur hunters began crossing the Bering Sea looking for sea otters in the Aleutian Archipelago. Their pelts fetched astronomical sums in trade with China, and a man of limited means could quickly amass a fortune. They quickly figured out that it was much more efficient to force the local Unangan men to do the hunting, and to this end they established a pattern of kidnapping wives and children and holding them as "guests," and paying for the skins the husbands brought in with a knife, a kettle, or a handful of beads. This was paltry restitution by any measure.

More and more hunters kept making the crossing throughout the 1700s, and the enterprise became consolidated into the hands of a few competing companies. By the 1780s, the hunters from these companies were fighting with each other as much as with Native people. In response to this, Czar Paul I forced a merger of the two most prominent companies, the Shelhikov-Golikov Company and the Lebedev-Lastochkin Company. The new enterprise was known as the Russian America Company—RAC for short—and became the de facto government of the colony.

For much of the 1800s, the Russian Empire was locked in a bitter struggle with the British Empire; they were the two largest empires the world has ever seen. Russia pushed eastward across Asia and into the continental lobe of North America that we now call Alaska. The British, through their proxy the Hudson Bay Company, pushed north and west across the lakes and rivers of Canada. The two empires collided at the 141st meridian, fixed as the boundary line by an international treaty in 1829.

Saint Michael, also known as Mikhailovski, was both a trading station and the Russian administrative seat of the lower Kwifpak/ Yukon River and Bering Sea coast. The posts of Nulato, Ikogmiut Mission, Unalakleet, and Andreivski all reported to the district manager at Saint Michael.

FROM MERIDIAN, BOOK THREE OF SEASONS OF WANT AND PLENTY

Two days later they came around a bend in the river and Maria sang out when she spied men sitting on the riverbank next to a beached bidara. "It's Russians?" she asked.

"I think it is," Kurila said. "Or at least, they're not Dinneh."

Lukin leaned on the tiller to point them in toward the shore across the wide current.

"My God," Anfisa whispered, squinting over her shoulder.

"What?" said Lukin.

"It's the bidara from Nulato."

Lukin stepped up onto the seat to gain a higher view. She was right. The boat had been dragged up onto the gravel with the crew propped against it sitting in a line. At first glance it seemed they were taking a smoke break or perhaps making repairs to the shell. Then they drew closer and he saw the arrows that filled their bodies and the bullet and axe wounds surrounded by the dried blood. At least two of them had their heads cut off. The bidara's shell had been chopped full of holes and was beyond repair.

"George," said Lukin with his eyes on the dead men, "I need you to ship your oar and load those repeating rifles."

Adams withdrew the four weapons they'd been keeping handy since leaving Nulato. Working quickly, he opened the buttplates and dropped seven cartridges into each magazine. As they steered into shore he set one loaded weapon before Rudnov and another next to Kurila, keeping each gun away from the swing of their oars as they pulled. He passed one to Lukin and he stood it against the transom as he leaned on the tiller. With the boat so heavily loaded they had to land out in the shallows. Adams splashed down over the side to secure the boat.

"Don't tie it up," Lukin said, "just hold the line so we can get out fast if we need to."

Adams nodded and slung his gun over his shoulder so he could hold the bow line with both hands.

Lukin took up his rifle. "Anatoli, you're with me. Kurila, stay here with the boat and keep your weapon handy." Kurila shipped his oar and took up the rifle. It was not lost on Lukin that he watched the forest rather than the massacre scene, for that was where trouble would come from if it came. The wildfire was still in the sky and there were low clouds above it. The air was dark and close with the atmosphere itself pressing in around them.

"It's definitely the Nulato crew," Rudinov said as they crept carefully in front the bodies. The cargo and guns were gone and they'd been there a couple of days from the look of them. Flies buzzed and crawled in and out of their noses to lay eggs. The sand and gravel of the bank had been churned up by a fight and there were black patches of blood where the men had fallen. It was obvious enough that they'd been dragged into position in front of the wrecked boat to send a message.

Lukin spotted a swallow tattoo on the arm of one of the headless corpses just below the rolled-up sleeve. "This is Shabunin?"

Rudinov stepped over and peered at the tattoo. "Yes."

"I'll give you three guesses who chopped his head off."

Rudinov's face was hard and flat. He pointed to the man next to Shabounin. His head was intact but a pair of steel-tipped arrows had been shot directly into his eyes at close range and left there protruding from the sockets with the fletchings propped into the sand between his thighs. "This man's name was Zakarov. He violated one of Larion's nieces a few months ago and said he'd cut her eyes out if she told anyone."

"Looks like he was still alive when it happened."

"You know who I don't see here?"

Lukin looked over the six corpses. "Captain Denisov."

Rudinov watched the forest with his rifle at the ready while Lukin moved around studying the marks on the ground. He saw what he was pretty sure were the tracks of at least a dozen Dinneh men—maybe twenty—coming onto the bank from the willows at a run. In a riot of lupine blooms he spotted a cloth patch that would have seated a musketball in the barrel, spat out and charred when the gun was fired. Then the scuffle of hand to hand combat closer to the water. There were the cold remains of a fire and a cheap kettle that had been knocked over and overlooked in the chaos.

"Looks like they were getting ready for a cup of tea," Rudinov said when Lukin joined him again in front of the bodies.

Lukin grunted. He could feel the others watching from the boat. "And Larion and Tikungah and their fighters came boiling out of the willows over there."

None of this was any great surprise, but it was the single pair of barefoot tracks he spotted down near the swirling edge of the water that caught his attention. It was the size and shape of a young girl, pressed into the damp sand. She hadn't been participating, but she'd been watching, and that was all the more disturbing. And then a man in Russian boots had come up and stood before her, toe to toe. Close enough to kiss her.

Rudinov saw it too. "There was only one man on this boat crew who would have been wearing Russian boots."

Lukin didn't move his eyes from the tracks. "Denisov. He was here."

About the Author

Kris Farmen is a writer, editor, and historian. His books include *The Devil's Share*, *Turn Again*, *Edge of Somewhere*, and *Blue Ticket*. His work has also appeared in *Alaska* magazine, the *Anchorage Press*, and *Russian Life*, among others. He lives in Alaska with his wife, daughter, and rescue dog.

Read more at https://www.krisfarmen.com/.

www.ingramcontent.com/pod-product-compliance
Ingram Content Group UK Ltd.
Pitfield, Milton Keynes, MK11 3LW, UK
UKHW042003190726
13854UKWH00005B/2141

9 798215 286371